I0537101

Her eyes sought him and reflected death . . . .

Wayne drew himself back from her seeking hands. He said huskily, "Where is Hake?"

"He doesn't matter," Priscilla murmured, still with closed eyes. "Kiss me, Morgan Wayne."

"He does matter." Wayne's voice was guttural with desire and with the driving determination that was in him. "Suppose he comes back?"

Her fingertips caressed his cheeks gently. "He would kill us both." Her voice was still a murmur. Without inflection. "Are you afraid of death? They say you're not. They say . . ."

"What do they say about me?" Wayne demanded roughly as her voice trailed off.

"Many things. And I believe them now. I've lived in fear so long, my dear. Hake loves death . . . for the sake of killing. Ugly and lingering death. He tells me at night. Gloats over it."

"So that's the way it is," said Wayne harshly. "Do you want to die, Priscilla?"

He walked a tightrope of danger, and beneath him they howled for his blood. . . .

THE AVENGER

by

Matthew Blood

WILDSIDE PRESS

Copyright 1952 by Fawcett Publications, Inc.

First Printing, April 1952

All Rights Reserved, Including the Right to
Reproduce This Book, or Portions Thereof.

THE AVENGER

Chapter One

IT WAS precisely four o'clock in the afternoon when Miss Lois Elling heard her employer returning from lunch. There was a solid wooden door at her left, and slightly behind her a side entrance to the old house that opened onto a small concrete porch and six concrete steps leading down to the driveway.

The door opened and Morgan Wayne entered the small room that had been turned into an office by setting up a typewriter desk in the center of it and a telephone stand beside the desk. There was also a straight chair for Miss Elling to sit in, and nothing else.

Wayne was bareheaded and immaculate in a creamy suit of heavy Irish linen, white-and-tan sports shoes, white shirt, and solid black four-in-hand tie. This seemed to be a sort of uniform with him. There had been no deviation

in a single article of clothing since Miss Elling had come
to work for him, though the white shirt was fresh each
morning, the suit neatly creased and spotless.

In many ways Morgan Wayne appeared to be a man
of definite and undeviating habit. He entered the door at
precisely nine-thirty each morning and said, "Good morn-·
ing," passing through the open door to the larger inner
room, where he seated himself in the comfortable swivel
chair behind the clean oak desk and laid the morning
Times out in front of him. He sat directly in Miss Elling's
line of vision through the open connecting door with his
left profile toward her. For a matter of five or ten minutes
each morning he sat perfectly motionless, looking fixedly
out the single, uncurtained window in the room. At the
end of that period he lit a cigarette and began reading
the paper. He appeared to read it carefully and with great
interest from the first page to the last—a task that required exactly two hours, with no more than a few minutes' leeway in either direction.

Thus, each morning it was approximately eleven-forty
by Miss Elling's watch when he laid aside his paper and
opened the top right-hand drawer of his desk and lifted
out a leather-covered pint flask and unscrewed the large
silver cap. He poured this to the brim with good bourbon
(Miss Elling knew it was good bourbon because she had
helped herself to a snifter from the flask during his lunch-
eon absence on her third day in his employ) and spent ten
minutes sipping the drink. The cap was then returned to
the flask and the flask to the drawer, and Morgan Wayne
would push back his swivel chair and get up. Moving
casually through the door to her office, he would pause
beside her desk and remark, "I think I'll go out to lunch
now, Miss Elling. You have yours, so you will be here to
take any messages?"

"Oh, yes, Mr. Wayne," she would tell him brightly,
"I'll be right here to take any messages."

Then Morgan Wayne would go out, and Miss Elling

would be alone until four o'clock, when he returned. As he was doing now. Pausing beside her desk to ask, "Nothing, Miss Elling?"

She shook her head and said, "Nothing, Mr. Wayne," and watched him go through the door to the swivel chair, where she knew he would sit until five o'clock, when he would turn his head and tell her pleasantly, "You may as well go along now, Miss Elling. Good night," and she would get up from her desk and say, "Good night, Mr. Wayne," and go out the door and down the concrete steps and out the driveway past his Cadillac convertible to the front of the old mansion on the height overlooking the parkway and the Flushing yacht basin, to walk the short distance to the subway station.

This was Thursday afternoon. Her fourth day on the job. During those four days, Morgan Wayne's routine had not varied. Thus far, he had spoken to Lois Elling exactly fifteen times since the first brief talk on Monday morning when she arrived with her card from the agency and he had explained that in the future he would expect her to bring a lunch she could eat in the office because there were no restaurants nearby and it would be necessary for her to be on hand in case there was a telephone call.

For four days now, the telephone had not rung once. There had been no callers at the two-room suite securely locked off from the rest of the seemingly deserted house.

There had been no dictation for Miss Elling to take, no letters for her to write. That first morning Wayne had gravely explained to her that she would be on trial for the first week, a sort of probationary period to see "how she worked out," as he had expressed it.

Well, she wondered viciously now, just how had she worked out? She glared at Morgan Wayne's profile through the open door as he seated himself in the swivel chair and asked herself for the thousandth time what in hell this rigmarole was all about.

In the beginning—that first day, at least—it had been

sort of exciting and fun to wonder about her new job and her new employer. To wait for him to do something, or give her something to do. To wonder what his business was, and why he had this queer sort of office set up in the two front rooms of this old deserted house overlooking the parkway. To wonder with a little tingle of frightened anticipation whether that closed door on the other side of his inner office opened into a luxuriously furnished love nest into which she would be initiated later.

After four days she still had vague ideas about the love nest beyond the closed door, but she knew it to be securely locked and had just about given up hopes of being invited inside.

And she knew no more about the nature of his business or why he required the services of a secretary than she had in the beginning. In the right-hand drawer of her typewriter desk reposed a full ream of printed letterheads. They said "Morgan Wayne" across the top. No address. No telephone number. No nothing. She knew it was a full, untouched ream, because the wide paper band encircling the sheets had not been broken.

In the left-hand drawer of her desk were five hundred large envelopes to match the printed stationery. On the back flap of each was the printed address of the house in which the office was located.

His name on the letterheads and an address on the envelopes.

There was also the bare, flat-topped desk in the inner room, with three drawers on each side and a shallow center drawer. Five of the side drawers were completely empty; the sixth held the leather-covered flask of good bourbon.

There was a checkbook in the shallow center drawer. Nothing else. A large, three-checks-to-the-page book with the name Morgan Wayne printed neatly at the top of each check. Three checks had been used, and the stubs were carefully filled in. The first check was dated less than a month previously, and the two following checks were each dated precisely one week later, on a Friday in each case (Miss Elling had checked the calendar with the dates to turn her first suspicion into a practical certainty).

She was thinking about those three checks as she sat rigidly at her desk a few minutes after four o'clock on Thursday afternoon and glared through the connecting door at her employer.

Morgan Wayne had seated himself comfortably in the swivel chair and was leaning back with both hands indolently clasped behind his head. From experience, Miss Elling knew he would hold that pose without moving for half an hour at least.

Her eyes were slightly glazed as she watched him across her typewriter, and she was thinking about those three checks—and that the next day would be Friday again.

She didn't really know she was going to do it when she felt her right hand going down to open the drawer of her desk. She kept watching Wayne fixedly as her fingers fumbled for the band of paper around the virgin ream and ripped it. The tearing sound was loud in the stillness, but Wayne did not twitch a muscle.

She still didn't know exactly what she was going to do when she lifted a sheet and slid it into the roller of her machine with trembling fingers.

Continuing to watch her employer's profile for some evidence of attention or interest, Miss Elling began typing rapidly. There was no reaction from the silent figure in the inner room. Her fingers flew over the keys nimbly and letters became words, and words became lines, and lines became paragraphs, while she kept on staring at Wayne with hypnotic intensity and allowed her subconscious mind to take over completely.

Who are you [she wrote]? What are you, Morgan Wayne? What sort of crazy setup is this? An office, you call it. In this old house away from everything. With a telephone that doesn't ring, a secretary who doesn't work . . . and you in your swivel chair!

How long do you think a girl can stand sitting here wondering? A week, huh? No more than that. You've got that one figured out. Is that why you fired the others after their "trial periods"? Or did they quit? That's what I'm wondering about right now. Because tomorrow is Friday again, you know, and I'm not going to quit, Morgan Wayne. So you'll have to fire me.

You see, I know about the others. That checkbook in your desk. Did you think for one moment that I wouldn't prowl around while you were out? Or didn't you care? Maybe you wanted me to look. To sort of be prepared for being fired tomorrow.

Three checks. Each for fifty dollars and each dated a succeeding Friday. To three different girls. Muriel Grane, Alice Hobbs, and Janice Neat. And tomorrow there'll be another stub. Another fifty dollars paid out to Lois Elling. For services rendered. *What* services? What services did Muriel and Alice and Janet render for their fifty bucks?

What about those other three girls, Mr. Wayne? My predecessors. Each one, I assume, hired for a one-week trial period, as I was. Were they surprised when you fired them at the end of one week? Why? Couldn't they handle the job? Weren't they efficient at sitting here in this chair and waiting for something to happen? Waiting for you to say something? To *do* something? Make a pass or some goddamn thing or other? How inefficient can a girl be at sitting in a chair and waiting?

How did you break the sad news to each of them, Morgan Wayne? How are you going to explain to me tomorrow afternoon that I simply haven't "worked out"?

Let's see, now. You will have to break down and actually say something to me, won't you? Something more than "Good morning" and "Good night." How will you do it, you big blond impervious self-satisfied bastard?

First I'll see you get out your checkbook and write in it. Then you'll come in and hand me my fifty bucks and you'll say:

"I'm extremely sorry, Miss Elling, but I'm afraid I'll have to let you go. The experiment simply hasn't been successful. You recall, of course, that this first week was a probationary period.

"You see, Miss Elling, I don't approve of your posture as you sit here and perform all the difficult and delicate tasks assigned to you. You simply don't sit still enough, Miss Elling. At four-twenty-six on Tuesday afternoon I observed you wriggling at your desk. And on Wednesday morning just before I went out to lunch you crossed your legs and then uncrossed them all in a matter of ten minutes.

"And, Miss Elling, the crowning horror of all—what actually convinced me that you simply would not do—was that disgusting performance of yours yesterday afternoon. I refer, of course, to your revolting effrontery in sitting here in plain view of me and typing a letter on one of my lovely letterheads.

"There must be silence in this office, Miss Elling. The clack of a typewriter simply *must not be*. I could set up my office in a mausoleum, of course, and obtain the same effect, but it would be difficult and probably expensive. And people might think it odd. I'll fire you instead and hire another secretary from another agency to report Monday morning. Perhaps *she* will fit my exacting specifications."

Is that what you will say to me, Mr. Morgan Wayne? Is that what you said to the others? Or will you come back from lunch tomorrow afternoon and go past me into your office and take a key out of your pocket and unlock that door leading into the interior of this old house and open the door and turn and say to me:

"All right, Miss Elling. Please step this way. This is my regular Friday-afternoon experiment to determine whether you will come back to work on Monday or whether I will have to try out another girl.

"That's correct, Miss Elling. Right this way. And take off your clothes, please. Everything, if you don't mind. To the last stitch. We're alone, you know. Quite alone in this old house. There's a comfortable bed in here. And champagne on ice. Soft lights and muted music. Just get out of your clothes, my dear, while I get out of mine. And then we'll see."

I wish you would do it that way, you big, blond Viking bastard. I might fool you, Morgan Wayne. Because I'd love it. What do you think of that? Go ahead and unlock your door and try me.

What in hell am I saying? I don't know. And I've reached the point where I don't care any more. You do that to a woman, you know. I bet you do know. Damn you. Damn you. *Damn* you. Just by walking past me and sitting there and saying nothing. Not even *looking* at me.

I'd make you look at me, damn your soul. I'd give you something to look at. Try me and see. I've got breasts, goddamn it, that tingle when I look at your big hands. Does that surprise you? I've got a smooth, flat, white stomach that cringes and does nip-ups inside when I look at the solid bulk of you sitting there in that chair. I've got strong thighs and a dimple in each knee.

So I'd *love* to be invited into your love nest, Morgan Wayne. I'd love to show you all that—and more. I'll call your bluff in a hurry if you unlock that door. Don't think you'll get rid of me so easily.

Did you frighten the others away? Muriel and Alice and Janet. Didn't one of them call your bluff? Or did they? And you still weren't satisfied, huh? They didn't have what it takes. Poor girls. I'm sorry for them, but then I'm glad, too, because if they hadn't all failed to

pass the test I wouldn't be sitting here waiting for you
to get up and unlock that door. . . .

Oh, my God! Am I going off my rocker completely?
How can this happen to me after just sitting here looking at you for four days? Damn you. Damn you. *Damn*
you. I'm Lois Elling. I'm thirty-two years old, unmar-
ried but not a virgin; moderately chaste but not a
prude. I've had men in my bed before. I can have any
one of half a dozen tonight if I like.

Nice guys, too. Not like you. Men who know what
women are built for—and are glad of it. All I have to
do is pick up the telephone to have one of them tonight.

But I won't, Morgan Wayne. Do you know what I'll
do tonight instead? What I've been doing every night
since I started working here.

I'll go home and take a bath. I'll lie in the steaming
hot tub and think about you. Wonder about you. *Want*
you. I'll wonder if you have my home telephone number, or whether you know it's in the book and all you
have to do is look under the E's and find me listed. And
I'll think about the telephone maybe ringing in the
other room and about jumping out of the tub and running in dripping to answer it and hearing your voice
over the wire. The voice I've heard just fifteen times
all told. And I'll lie in the hot tub and dream about
standing there stupidly, dripping water on the white
rug in front of the telephone and asking you in my most
ladylike voice how soon you can get there. And dropping the phone and hurrying like hell to dry myself
and powder myself and dab on just a touch of perfume
and going into the bedroom shaky all over and kneeling
down to open the bottom bureau drawer and digging
all the way down to the bottom and getting out the
tissue-wrapped black negligee that Bill Johnson gave
me for Christmas five years ago and that I've never
worn. I'd have worn it for Bill, you can bet, but he was
killed in an auto accident two days before Christmas

and I haven't met another man since for whom I wanted to wear it.

Until I met you.

That's what I'll do tonight, Morgan Wayne. . . .

The telephone rang at Miss Lois Elling's right hand. She jumped as though aroused from deep sleep and looked at the instrument in dazed disbelief. It couldn't be. It wasn't supposed to ring. It wasn't a real telephone. Just a stage prop, like Morgan Wayne himself and the typewriter and the unused letterheads.

It rang again. Just like any other telephone. In a demanding and businesslike way. She turned her chair to lift the instrument and speak into the mouthpiece. She listened intently, frowning in concentration, then slowly replaced the receiver on its prongs and turned back to see Wayne standing beside her.

He had moved as swiftly and as silently as a stalking tiger, and he stood beside her chair looking down at the typed words in her machine.

Momentarily Miss Elling's office training held sway over her mind and she was the crisply efficient secretary she had always been in the past.

"A message for you, Mr. Wayne. And he hung up. He said . . . Oh, my God!" Realization stabbed at her, brought the breathless exclamation to her lips and flaming color to her cheeks.

Morgan Wayne was standing there calmly reading what she had written in her bemused state of almost complete unconsciousness. Her hand clawed out at the typewritten page, but Wayne's fingers closed over her wrist effortlessly, pressed her back into her chair while his eyes raced over the typed words.

A muscle twitched in the right side of his mouth while Miss Elling moaned in an agony of embarrassment and fought against his strength to reach past him and retrieve the sheet.

He released her wrist as abruptly as he had grabbed it, shaking his head slowly and turning amused blue eyes on her. She cringed back in her chair away from him, tight-lipped and crimson and panting with anger and humiliation, wilting before the hot flame she saw lurking in the icy depths of his eyes.

He said, "The message, Miss Elling?"

She averted her head wildly, flinging both hands up to her face to hide it from him, moaning tremulously through tight lips.

"Please." His voice was tolerant and reasonable, yet with an added note of curtness. "You did get the message?"

She nodded her head slowly, keeping her face turned away and covered with her hands. Her voice was muffled and thin as she forced herself to say, "Tell Wayne they jumped the gun and grabbed Letty ten minutes ago on the Sawmill River Parkway. I lost them headed for town."

Wayne stood motionless and silent. Miss Elling held her breath for a long moment, expelled it with a shuddering sigh, and dared to steal a glance at him through outspread fingers.

He stood close beside her, but his head was lifted and he was looking over her head. His face was taut and hard, and there was a look about him of listening, of waiting tensely for some signal.

He had forgotten her, she thought. He stood there beside her chair after reading her nymphomaniacal ravings and was as unaware of her as though she did not exist.

He turned abruptly without a downward glance and strode to his inner office, where he looked searchingly out the window again. Somehow, Wayne's indolent manner had vanished. There was a sudden impression of terrific leashed power in every movement and in his stance before the window.

It didn't mean anything to him, she thought wildly. He doesn't care what I wrote. I needn't be ashamed at all. He doesn't *care*. She bit her underlip until a drop of blood spurted from it, reached forward listlessly to rip the sheet from her typewriter and tear it into tiny fragments.

She was standing up with her back to the room, reaching up with trembling fingers for an absurd concoction of feathers and ribbon that hung on the wall when Wayne's voice sounded immediately behind her with the purring timbre of a jungle cat. "What are you doing, Miss Elling? It isn't quitting time."

She stood with her back turned, her slender body rigid. "Oh, yes, it is." Her voice trembled and she hated herself for that. "I'm leaving. I've had quite enough of this job."

She made herself lift the hat from its hook on the wall, and it fell from nerveless fingers to the floor when his fingers lightly touched the right side of her neck where the flesh flowed down smoothly into the shoulder.

"I need you, Lois." His voice caressed her. She fought against the weakness, against the flame that crept over her body with the touch of his fingers against her flesh, the sound of his voice only inches from her ear.

"This is it, darling. Don't you see?" His fingers put pressure on the side of her neck, turning her head so that she looked into the hot glow from Morgan Wayne's eyes. "Call this number I've left on your desk." His voice had a hypnotic quality that soothed and embraced her. "Get Julius Hendrixon. He must call me at once. As soon as he gets any word whatever. The moment it comes. Day or night. Don't leave this phone until six. Then go home fast and stay there for a message. Give Hendrixon your number."

"And where . . . can I reach you later?" The words came out flatly and Miss Elling was scarcely conscious of speaking them.

"Where do you think—after that letter you wrote me?" His eyes held hers and strength flowed out of her body. "Take your hot bath, Lois, and open that bottom bureau drawer . . . and wait for me."

He was gone then. And Miss Elling slumped back against the wall and watched him go. Her mouth opened and closed slowly half a dozen times but no words came out.

She pushed herself erect after a time, pressed the knuckles of doubled fists to her forehead, and shook her head back and forth dazedly. Then, moving like a sleep-walker, she sat at her desk to dial the number he had left for her, and to deliver his cryptic message to a man named Julius Hendrixon.

Chapter Two

EXACTLY twenty minutes later, Morgan Wayne's convertible wheeled up to the curb in front of a cellar joint on Fifty-second Street that said "Gingham Gardens" over the cave door.

It was too early for the neons, but the life-sized oil painting of a long-stemmed doll in lacy bra and G-string with gingham parasol coyly poised above her head had been wheeled out in front to attract the early suckers. And the doorman was operating his clip. He strolled across the sidewalk with shoulders bursting from his fancy monkey suit, shaking his head sternly under a three-cornered headpiece of gingham.

"No parking here, sir. You'll have to . . ."

Wayne opened the door and got out. He said pleasantly, "Watch my car, will you? And take care of any cops." Somehow there was a ten-dollar bill in his hand, and somehow it disappeared, and the doorman said, "Certainly, sir," to his back as he went down three steps to the dim foyer.

The hat-check girl was a languid blonde. Her smile had a frozen, tailored quality, and mascaraed eyebrows arched upward haughtily when she saw he was hatless.

Wayne moved toward her slowly and smiled with a shake of his head. "It's not that way at all, honey. I'm not ducking the pay-off, it's just that I don't like hats." This time the bill between his fingers was a five. She appeared not to notice it as she took all of him in. Her eyes began to glow and the tailored quality vanished from her smile. She leaned a little forward so the counter pushed lush breasts up even more revealingly inside the georgette blouse and assured him, "On you, no hat looks O.K. to me."

She had long, smooth fingers with nails lacquered ruby red. The tips were warm and they pulsed against his hand as they took the bill. Wayne leaned one elbow on the counter and studied the interior decorations of the thin blouse with appreciation. He asked, "Anybody around?" scarcely moving his lips and keeping his eyes hooded.

She wriggled a trifle and moved closer, bathing him in body warmth and perfume. "Don't you like what you've seen this far?"

He said, "I've seen worse in my time." He lifted his gaze slowly, catching the smooth line of her throat, the pouting mouth that was close to his with the wet tip of tongue just inside, the brown eyes that opened a little wider as he met them and glowed with open invitation.

She said, "I'm off in a couple of hours."

He said, "I'll keep that in mind." He trailed the tips of his fingers across her bare forearm, let his smile widen into a grin, and turned inside.

The Gingham Gardens was typical of this block on Fifty-second. Long and narrow and dark. Red gingham paper on the walls. Blue gingham cloths on the tiny round tables. Accent on sweet simplicity to make the corn-and-cotton-belt boys feel at home. Sweet simplicity fronting for every sort of loathsome vice in the big town.

The back bar was lighted at this lull before the cocktail hour, and down at the other end of the room a bucket lamp threw a yellow glow where the hot-piano man was fingering some arrangements.

Wayne turned in to the deserted bar and the beefy bartender came alive. "What's yours, Mac?"

Wayne knew that bar rye was what you got in a joint like this no matter what you ordered, so he didn't mince matters.

"Bar rye and soda."

It came in a heavy glass thimble that nicked him ninety cents. Wayne carefully gathered up the dime left from his bill and pocketed it, smiling gently at the glowering look this action earned from the bartender. He dribbled the drops of whisky over ice cubes in his highball glass and asked casually, "Anybody around?"

The bartender rested a chunky forearm on the bar and shook his bullet head slowly. "Only a cheapskate dropping in from the street now and then."

Wayne didn't say anything. He carefully poured soda in his glass, swished it negligently for a moment, then threw the contents of the glass in the man's beefy face.

The man ducked and sputtered, swiping at his face with a bar rag and stooping to reach beneath the bar.

Morgan Wayne didn't alter his casual posture. He said, "I wouldn't," and something in his voice jerked the man to a halt before he came erect.

Their eyes locked across the bar and the chill blue of Wayne's drilled into the veined milkiness of the other's. "I asked," Wayne reminded him, "if anybody was around."

"Trouble, Pete?"

The voice came from behind Wayne's right shoulder. He turned casually. A man had emerged from the sick dimness of the rear. He wasn't big like the barman. He didn't even look tough. But in the half-light from behind the bar he exuded menace. Maybe it was his eyes.

His hair was slick and black. A slight figure and a boyish face. All but the eyes. They weren't boyish. They weren't anything you could describe. Holes for him to see through. Mirroring nothing. No imagination, no feelings. Nothing.

He stood hard on the heels of two-toned Oxfords, hands thrust deep in the slanting pockets of a tan sports jacket. He could be holding a pocket gun. At any rate, Wayne caught the bulge of a shoulder rig that the carefully tailored jacket had been built to hide.

"Bastard got nasty and trun his glass at me," the bartender sputtered. "You want I should—"

"Shut up, Pete." The man's voice was like his eyes:

flat and devoid of expression, yet somehow imbued with the reptilian menace of a Gila monster. He didn't look at the bartender as he spoke. He asked Wayne:

"Why?"

Wayne shrugged. He was leaning sideways with one elbow on the bar. He said, "Tell your boss Morgan Wayne is here."

"Will that make him clap his hands?"

"Try it, Sutra. Or should I call you Willie?"

"Where'd you get my name?"

"Saw you on TV. Don't you know you're famous, Willie, since your testimony in front of Kefauver? About how you think the drug traffic stinks and no decent crook should sell the stuff to kids."

The trace of a smirk appeared on Willie Sutra's face. "No kiddin'? I done that good, huh?"

Wayne sighed. He said, "Nuts to this." He looked over Willie's head to the end of the long room, where a girl was now standing in the pool of light over the piano. She was looking at Wayne, humming softly while the piano player soft-keyed. She was tall and slender and impossibly lovely, and at thirty feet her gaze had an impact that hit a man in the midriff. Her eyes held Wayne's and she kept on humming softly. He straightened slowly and moved away from the bar in her direction.

Willie Sutra was in his way. Willie didn't move. He spoke in a voice so soft it was barely audible. "The other way is out."

Wayne paused, wrenching his gaze away from the girl with an effort to look down consideringly at the little man. "I don't think the boss would like seeing the floor all messy with blood." His tone was almost as soft as Willie's. "Your blood."

He started forward and this time Willie stepped aside.

Wayne paid no more attention to him. He was headed for the girl standing in the soft pool of light beside the piano. He didn't know what he was going to say to her when he got there, but he knew she was in it somehow. The key to the whole situation was here. If she had it, she would give it to him. He knew that with certainty as he moved slowly toward her.

It happens that way sometimes. You look at a girl and she looks at you and you both know how it is, how it has to be. How it's going to be if you both have to tear down . a dozen stone walls to make it so.

It was more than just desire. Hell, you could desire a sexy twerp like the hat-check girl. Call it lust if you like. That's a good four-letter word. No matter what name you give it, Wayne knew he had been clubbed.

Maybe because she seemed so out of character here. You wouldn't think a girl in a cellar joint could look demure, but this one did. You looked at her once across thirty feet of dimness and you thought of everything the hat-check girl made you think of. But you also thought of home and mother. Climbing rosebushes and a white cottage with lighted windows.

Her dress matched the gingham décor of the place. A material of small green checks that looked like gingham, but had the radiance of silk. A wide neck, but not immodestly low. An old-fashioned bodice hugging her incredibly slender waist, giving her breasts what you knew was an unbrassiered uplift that made you think of a pair of hands cupped beneath them. Your hands. But on her it wasn't lewd, somehow. Beneath the bodice, a wide skirt flared to just below her knees. If she moved fast you'd expect it to show flashes of a peek-a-boo petticoat playing tag with sheer nylons.

Wayne was close to her now. She had stopped humming and was just standing there. Watching him. He didn't know what he was going to say. But he didn't think it was going to be difficult to get started.

It wasn't. She cued him with coolly perfect lips that had been lightly touched with pale lipstick that hadn't ruined the contour:

"Don't look now, mister, but I think you're being followed."

Wayne stopped in front of her. He didn't look around. He said, "Tell him to go away."

She said, "Go away, Willie." Her eyes smiled at Wayne.

Wayne had always thought that only girls in fiction had green eyes. But this girl was real. And her eyes were green. Limpid sea green, with bluish depths that invited him to sink into them and drown deliciously. Wayne did a double take on that one. When you begin to get lyrical about a cellar wren's eyes . . .

But, goddamnit, they were green. Limpid sea green. With bluish depths. . . .

A cold kill with her red hair. Because the hair wasn't just red. It was *unbelievably* red. But you wanted to believe it. On her it was easy to believe. Pouring in a smooth flow to her shoulders, alive and vibrant and with a tinge of gold. It couldn't be real, but you knew it was.

He heard Willie Sutra's voice behind him, disappointed and sullen: "But this here goop—"

"I said to go away, Willie."

Wayne lifted his gaze to her face again. "They've got the wrong girl in the picture outside."

She made a bashful-girl curtsy, and an honest-to-God dimple dented her left cheek. "Thank you, sir, she said. But don't you think it might be a mite egotistical, since I own the joint? Pardon me—my highly paid promotion man is trying to teach me to call it an establishment."

"My God," said Wayne softly. "Of course. The Gingham Girl, they called you when you first turned up as a warbler for Lon Kagle's band. And six months later you ended up by owning the joint. Pardon me, Miss Endicott. Establishment."

"Sordid success story, isn't it?" She smiled like a little girl explaining away childish mischief. "And why don't you call me Priscilla?"

Wayne's blue eyes were hooded now, his strong face set

in lines of harshness. "My God," he said again, more softly now, "I'm beginning to remember . . . a lot of things."

"And?" Her chin was lifted proudly and he saw a pulse leaping at the base of her lovely throat.

"Hake Derr." He pronounced the two words slowly, as though tasting them dubiously. He shook his head briefly and angrily and looked into her eyes again. "Do you know what you did to me, Priscilla? When I walked across the room to you?"

Her slender body stiffened as though to defend itself against physical onslaught. The piano man was hunched on his stool half turned from them, cigarette drooping from slack lips, loose fingers brushing the keys softly as though seeking an unborn melody.

Priscilla Endicott said, "Yes." She paused, lowering golden lashes and catching a seductive lower lip inde-cisively between her teeth in maidenly embarrassment, or the best facsimile of it that Wayne had ever witnessed. "The same thing you did to me." Her voice was a whisper, throaty and full of promise.

He steeled himself against it. This was Priscilla Endi-cott! And there were the rumors about Hake Derr. About other men, too, but none of them mattered. Hake Derr did matter.

Wayne moved closer to her. He said, "But it's too late for that. Isn't it, Priscilla?" He put urgency into the ques-tion.

She lifted her lashes to invite him again to drown in the bluish depths of her limpid green eyes. "Is it ever too late for that . . . between a man like you and a woman like me?"

Wayne reached forward to touch the cold fingers of her hand, which rested on the piano. He said gently, "I'm Morgan Wayne."

A convulsive tremor rippled through her taut body. Her fingers tightened into a fist beneath his hand. He knew the name meant something to her—knew he was on the right track. The key was here. She could give it to him, if . . .

She said slowly, "You came here looking for Hake?"

"And found the most beautiful woman in the world."

She shuddered and closed her eyes. "Go away, Morgan Wayne. Fast. Don't ever come back."

"Then it's true?"

"What?"

"What they say about Hake Derr . . . and the Gingham Girl."

"Yes." She opened her eyes and attempted a derisive smile. It wasn't a good effort. It ended up in a pitiful appeal that tore at his heart. Again, he wondered whether she could be that good an actress.

She tightened her lips and made her voice hard. "So you see why you'd better beat it fast, Morgan Wayne."

He shook his head. His voice remained gentle, but there was a thread of steel in it. "I'm not very good at running. I won't until you say *you* want me to, Priscilla . . . privately."

She appeared to go listless then. She withdrew her fingers from beneath his hand and straightened with a suggestion of a shrug. Perhaps it was a shrug of defiance, or of desperation.

"Perhaps I had better tell you . . . privately."

She moved away from him and Wayne followed her. The piano player did not lift his head as they passed behind him. His fingers continued to brush the keys lightly and the haunting sound followed them down a corridor to a flight of narrow stairs that led upward.

Priscilla Endicott climbed the stairs unhesitatingly. There is something about a woman going up a stairway and a lone man close behind her. Something for both of them. Disturbingly intimate. Something atavistic, perhaps. Buried deep in the subconscious of both. An intimate awareness of each other and of animal instincts that have been glossed over and submerged by centuries of civilization. Yet never wiped out. Still the dominant instinct in man and woman.

As he followed Priscilla closely on the stairway, Wayne's face remained level with her moving loins. Her woman perfume came back to him in a warm wave, and there was the rustle of her taffeta skirt. Something, always, between a man and a woman climbing single file on a narrow stairway.

Climbing upward to . . . what?

Morgan Wayne didn't know. Probably to an apartment she shared with Hake Derr. Quite possibly to meet Hake himself.

It didn't matter. Right now, it didn't. There were the two of them climbing a narrow stairway. There was the smell of her, and the proud tilt of her head, and the small movements of her buttocks so close to his face.

They reached the top of the stairway, and still without a backward glance or a spoken word Priscilla unlocked a door and crossed the threshold. Morgan Wayne followed her without hesitation.

Chapter Three

Priscilla Endicott stopped in the center of the long room and stood there without turning her head. Wayne closed the door quietly and stood with his back against it, taking in vague details of the pleasant warmth of the room while his gaze was riveted on the tall, gingham-clad figure standing so utterly motionless before him.

Priscilla's hands hung limply by her sides. Somehow, there was hopelessness and uncertainty in her stance. She was waiting—and Morgan Wayne waited. He felt his pulse leaping uncontrollably, and was suddenly aware that he was holding his breath.

It was Priscilla's room, warm and alive with color and pattern. Chartreuse draperies hung low to the floor from a wide window at the far end. The room was thickly carpeted from wall to wall with a pattern of dull reds and yellows, and not cluttered with furniture.

But it was cluttered with a man's white shirt lying rumpled and conspicuous just inside an open door leading into the bedroom. Hake Derr's shirt! A mute reminder to Wayne that he was alone here with another man's woman.

Past the rumpled shirt and through the open door, Wayne could see half an oversized Hollywood bed with the covers thrown back, one pillow and the sheet wrinkled. Past the bed was a low, glass-topped vanity almost bare on top. Cut-glass stoppered flagons and powder container on one side; a pair of silver-topped military brushes on the other.

Another mute reminder of Hake Derr. And there was a third. From where he stood, the large oval mirror above the vanity reflected its glass-topped surface. There was a light sprinkling of powder over the center area and the mirror reflected the four letters of an obscene word evidently scrawled by a blunt fingertip in the powder; scrawled on the top of Priscilla Endicott's dressing table by a man with the puerile mind of a nasty adolescent who has just learned a new word. You see it furtively scrawled sometimes on city sidewalks and on the white walls of a latrine.

Morgan Wayne felt sudden and inexpressible pity for Priscilla.

Priscilla still stood motionless with her back toward him. But the fingers of both hands began to tighten into fists by her side. They relaxed and tightened again. Then they were lifted savagely to both sides of her head, finger-tips thrusting into the silken strands of her incredibly lovely hair and mussing it as Wayne's fingers longed to muss it.

She turned to him like that, and her face was pinched and bloodless, haunted with terror and with passion. Her breath came fast between tight lips and her breasts rose and fell rapidly.

She stared at him for a long moment as though it were the first time she had seen his face.

She said, "Are you going to take me?" and it was spoken as casually as though she had asked, "Would you like a drink?"

Wayne moved toward her across the heavy carpet, his eyes searching her face. When they were close enough he saw the perspiration of excitement wetting her temples, the pulsing tremors in the rounded softness of her throat beneath the lifted chin; could feel the hot breath coming to him from slightly parted lips.

Morgan Wayne put out his hands to grip her shoulders. He drew her toward him and she did not resist. He looked down into her eyes and knew that if he kissed her he was lost. Not yet. There was something more important than this woman, but it was difficult to remember what it was. Damned difficult. Almost impossible. Every cell in his body leaped in response to her, every fiber of his being strained to get closer.

His teeth were set together so tightly that his jaws ached and he exerted every atom of will power he possessed to turn his head slightly from her and look down at the rumpled shirt on the floor. He didn't realize the strength of his grip on her shoulders as he demanded hoarsely, "What about Hake Derr?"

That name broke the spell. He felt the rigidity of Priscilla's body go away under his fingers. She turned her head also and looked where he was looking. His hands fell away from her shoulders and she moved listlessly to pick up the shirt. Over her shoulder she said:

"You were right downstairs. It is too late." She moved into the bedroom, balling the shirt up in her two hands and then tossing it casually into a corner.

Wayne followed her to the doorway. Every sense was alert now. Every moment was important. He had to re-capture some of the essence of the moment before, yet not enough to be trapped by it. God knew, a man could be trapped by it easily enough. For one moment back there . . .

She stopped in front of the low vanity. From across the room, Morgan Wayne heard the swift intake of her breath, saw the swift movement of her hand that wiped out the four letters on the powder-strewn glass.

She turned to face him, leaning back with hips against the table edge, supporting herself with hands on both sides of her. She looked tired now, almost contemptuous.

"Why don't you get out, Morgan Wayne? Of course it's too late . . . for you."

"You lie, Priscilla," Wayne told her. "You lie most foully in your beautiful teeth. You asked me a question a while ago. You didn't have to ask it. You already knew the answer. You knew it when you looked at me as you stood at the piano and I was at the bar. The only question is when. For us it has to be right." His voice was insistent. Urgent and demanding. Speaking with a quiet logic and a certainty that again ripped away the barrier that had risen between them. "You know that, Priscilla." Wayne began to move across the bedroom toward her.

She didn't respond. Not yet. She still looked tired, but the expression of contempt was beginning to be replaced by one of speculation. She lowered her lashes and ran the tip of her tongue around dry lips.

"Who are you?"

He halted two feet in front of her. "Morgan Wayne."

"But *what* are you?" Her lashes remained lowered but the words burst from her lips as though long pent up.

"Ask Hake Derr."

"He doesn't know. Only hints about you here and there. Rumors that you're this and that. For God's sake," she pleaded wildly, and she lifted her lashes and showed actual wetness in the limpid green eyes, "go away from here. Stay away from Hake. I'll follow you. I'll come wherever you say. Whenever you send for me."

The wetness was tears. They streamed down her cheeks unashamedly. Wayne took one step forward and put his arm about her shaking shoulders. She twisted her face away from him. Her teeth were chattering and she crushed the knuckles of one hand against them.

Wayne pulled the hand away roughly. He twisted her head so her mouth came up to meet his. It was a savage kiss. Her breasts were crushed against him and both arms clung desperately about his neck and a low moan escaped from her set teeth. Her head fell back away from him limply and her eyes were closed, her face peaceful now with a strange look of content.

She said, "Yes, darling. Yes! But hurry. I have no shame left. No fear. Nothing. Hurry, my dear. Oh, God! *Hurry.*"

A shudder traversed the length of her body. She opened her eyes to his gaze and there was a little-girl pleading in them. A surprised and almost virginal look of ecstasy.

Wayne turned to lower her unresisting body onto the unmade bed. She lay back limply and closed her eyes again. A tremulous smile fluttered across her lips. Wayne lay beside her and lowered his face within inches of hers. She lay with eyes closed, quiescent and waiting, only the gradual increase in the tempo of her breathing betraying the inner excitement gripping her.

Wayne kissed each eyelid gently. He moved his mouth down a tear-wet cheek to the slightly parted lips and across them. She began to shudder again and her hands reached for him.

Wayne drew himself back from her seeking hands. He said huskily, "Where is Hake?"

"He doesn't matter," Priscilla murmured, still with closed eyes. "Kiss me, Morgan Wayne."

"He does matter." Wayne's voice was guttural with desire and with the driving determination that was in him. "Suppose he comes back . . . to get his shirt?"

Her fingertips caressed his cheeks gently. "He would kill us both." Her voice was still a murmur. Without inflection. Uncaring and unafraid. "Are you afraid of death? They say you're not. They say . . ."

"What do they say about me?" Wayne demanded roughly as her voice trailed off.

"Many things. And I believe them now. I've lived in fear so long, my dear. You can't know. Hake Derr isn't human. He loves death . . . for the sake of killing. Ugly and lingering death. He tells me at night. Gloats over it."

"That," said Wayne harshly, "is what I thought. Do you want to die, Priscilla?"

"I don't think I care. Take me in your arms." Her voice was dreamy now, languid and peaceful as the sea after a violent storm has abated.

Morgan Wayne sat up angrily. He made his voice even more harsh. "Come out of it, Priscilla. I might be willing to trade my life for half an hour in bed with you, but by

God, I want to be assured of that half hour. Where is Derr at this moment?"

"Where it would take him more than half an hour to get here. Do you have to waste time with questions?"

"Yes," he said savagely. "Until I *know*." He reached forward and lifted the French telephone from a low stand beside the bed and held it close to her face. "Here."

"What's that?" She opened her eyes and looked dazedly at the phone as though she had never seen one before.

"A telephone," he said patiently.

"What for?"

"To check on Hake Derr. If he's where you think—if we have got that half hour—then we'll have it."

She sat up slowly, as though emerging from a hypnotic trance. "Suppose Hake isn't there?"

"Then we get the hell out of here—fast."

She sighed and took the telephone. She suddenly seemed to come alive to full awareness of the situation again, and gave him a nervous smile that was almost a hoyden's grin.

"I guess that does make sense. What'll I say?"

"Anything. Just to make sure he's there."

"I'll have to say something about your being here. Willie will tell him."

Wayne shrugged and reached for a cigarette. "Play it straight. Tell him I was here and frightened you."

Priscilla Endicott drew in a deep breath and dialed a number. Wayne was lighting his cigarette and appeared uninterested, but he watched her finger with concentration and etched the numbers in his mind.

She said, "Hello," into the mouthpiece, her voice unconsciously becoming hushed and guarded. "That you, Al? Priscilla. Let me talk to Hake."

She listened a moment, then said forcibly, "I know all that, but this is important. Put Hake on."

She cradled the mouthpiece hard against the valley between her breasts and told Wayne in a low voice, "He's there, all right. I'll tell him you've already gone and—"

There was a rasping sound from the earpiece and she lifted it swiftly. Morgan Wayne drew deeply on his cigarette and attempted to look at her dispassionately. How much of all this had been an act? How much of it honest emotion? Before God, he didn't know. Was she aware that when you pressed the mouthpiece of a telephone against your diaphragm and spoke even in a low voice, the words were transmitted over the wire by vibration just as clearly as though you spoke into the mouthpiece?

If she was aware of that, then she might as well have shouted to a jealous man that there was someone else in her bedroom with her and he'd better get there fast.

If she didn't know about that vibration thing, of course . . .

Her voice was dulcet in the mouthpiece: "Hake, honey. Listen. A man named Morgan Wayne was here looking for you . . . I *know,* honey, I've heard you mention him. I suckered him upstairs here thinking I might hold him till you came, but he got cagey and beat it. Thought I'd better call you right away . . . Sure, honey. See you tonight." She cradled the phone and turned exultantly. "He won't be here for hours, so let's—"

She broke off with a swift intake of breath as Morgan Wayne swung to his feet. He had what he needed now, and his face was grim. Whether Priscilla knew it or not, Hake Derr knew there was someone in her bedroom with her while she phoned. Besides that, every moment was precious now. Letty was just a youngster. Anything might be happening to her, and he had a telephone number.

He stood looking down at her and Priscilla shrank from what she saw in his face.

"Believe it or not, my sweet, I just remembered a date with my secretary. It can't wait, so *we'll* have to."

He swung on his heel and strode away fast, carrying with him the memory of the stricken look on the most beautiful face he had ever seen.

He didn't look back at Priscilla. He knew he might turn back to her if he did.

He heard her swearing at him as he went through the living room. He slammed the door behind him and went down the stairs two at a time, slowed as he reached the bottom, and moved casually out into the club, which was beginning to fill up now and hum with evening activity.

He didn't see Willie Sutra, and passed by the bartender swiftly with face averted. The hat-check girl leaned forward expectantly when she saw him, but Wayne waggled two fingers at her and kept going.

His convertible was still at the curb and without a parking ticket. The doorman was busy helping a tipsy party of four from a cab, and Wayne went behind his back and pushed out into the traffic.

He drove expertly and swiftly to the first empty space at the curb in front of a blue telephone sign. He sprinted in and used a dime to dial a certain number. When a gruff voice answered, he said:

"Morgan Wayne, John. Get me an address to match this telephone number fast." He repeated the number Priscilla Endicott had dialed and said impatiently, "It's goddamned important. Of course I'll hang on."

He waited with the receiver to his ear, blue eyes hooded and hard as they stared out of the booth, seeing Priscilla's face floating before him, hearing her voice again in his ears.

Then the gruff voice was speaking over the wire, and he memorized the address that went with the telephone number. He said, "Got it, John. Thanks," and hung up. He hurried back to his car and slammed out into New York's evening traffic again.

Chapter Four

Hake Derr lowered the telephone gently to its cradle. He stood without moving for a moment, thick shoulders hunched forward slightly, straining the seams of his carefully tailored tweed jacket. He had smooth, chubby features with a deep cleft in his chin that gave him a deceptive look of almost innocent boyishness. Until you looked into his eyes. They were neither innocent nor boyish. Nor were they cold or lifeless like Willie Sutra's.

Hake Derr's eyes were round and slightly protuberant. They were such a light gray as to appear almost white— an effect that was heightened by fragmentary brows so close to flesh color that they were practically invisible. The result was curious and somehow frightening.

You looked into Hake Derr's eyes and saw mirrored there such depths of depravity that you shuddered involuntarily. They were old with sin and with hatred for his fellow men. More than mere hatred, for that can be clean; there was bitterness and revulsion that encompassed all of humanity.

Derr pursed his thick lips and made a faint sucking sound as though he tasted something good. This was it. Morgan Wayne had finally come into the open. So he was real. All those vague rumors that had come to Derr's ears recently had a solid foundation.

Letty Hendrixon's snatch had forced Wayne to make an overt move. It was all right now. There was no great hurry. Wayne would keep all right. Set up for the kill in Priscilla's apartment. Those whispered words that had vibrated over the wire to Derr's ear were assurance that Morgan Wayne would be with her for some little time, at least. "He's there, all right. I'll tell him you've already gone and—"

Yeah, Priscilla was all right. And smart, too. Pressing the mouthpiece hard against her chest while she lured Wayne in a passion-laden voice to take his time and pleasure with her after checking to be sure her lover wasn't likely to interrupt for a few hours.

Sure. Priscilla was O.K. But was she as smart as he was thinking? A tiny doubt gnawed at Hake Derr's mind. *Did* she know that trick about bone conduction sending words over the telephone when the instrument was smothered against your body?

Wait a minute now. Maybe not. It wasn't common knowledge. If she hadn't done it intentionally, it meant she was actually two-timing Derr instead of Wayne. It meant she was up there in bed with him right now—and liking it, goddamn it. Not setting him up for the kill, but painting a large pair of horns right on Hake Derr's forehead.

That made a difference. One hell of a difference. Derr could accept and applaud the idea of a woman taking a man to bed with her to hold him until her lover could get there to handle the situation, but a wave of red-hot jealousy swept over him with the other thought. He didn't mind how many men she had as a matter of business, but not, by God, for any other reason.

He turned away from the telephone slowly, and Al, who was lounging in the bedroom doorway after taking the call, caught a glimpse of that jealousy in the momentary spasm that contracted Derr's face.

Al was slender and dark and foppish, and now he smirked knowingly. "That Gingham Gal! She really does go for you, Boss, but sometimes I get to wondering if you really do get it all."

Ordinarily Hake Derr would have shrugged off the remark. But ordinarily he was sure he was getting it all. Now that tiny doubt was gnawing at him.

His smooth, boyish face was blandly impassive as he neared Al. He smiled faintly and said without rancor,

"You shouldn't ought to think dirty like that." His left hand came out of his coat pocket with brass knuckles over the fingers and they smashed cruelly and without warning into the middle of Al's grin. He staggered back with blood spurting from his mouth, choking over half a dozen front teeth driven back into his throat.

Derr brushed past him casually, explaining, "If you do think it, next time you won't be so quick to say it."

He stopped on the threshold of the small bedroom and dispassionately removed the knuckles and dropped them back into his pocket. It was an ordinary bedroom with the sort of furniture that comes with a rented house. The gray light of late afternoon came through a single window to illuminate the bed on which the girl lay.

She lay on her side with her face toward Derr, twisting and straining futilely against the belt buckled about her knees and the length of clothesline that bound her wrists behind her back. A bathroom sponge was jammed into her mouth for a gag, held in place by a soiled handkerchief bound around her head.

Disheveled dark hair was splayed about her face, and one brown eye blazed with anger at Derr and the other man in the room, who leaned negligently against the opposite wall, idly chewing on a matchstick and watching her struggles with the impersonal interest of a scientist observing an impaled specimen.

Her face was pale and thin and she looked like a sophomore in high school, but the breast that had escaped from the ripped print dress and lay exposed on the counterpane was as round and full as that of a mature woman.

The man leaning against the wall moved his head a fraction of an inch in her direction and spoke past the matchstick between his teeth. "Some nice stuff there, Chief. You want me and Al to unbuckle that belt?"

Derr said dispassionately, "She's sixteen years old, you fool."

"Hell of a build for sixteen." Charlie straightened up and yawned. "Way she yammered at Al and me in the car 'fore we slapped that sponge in her mouth, she figgered we'd grabbed her for some sport and wasn't fighting too hard to get away."

Hake Derr moved forward two steps and looked down at the girl speculatively. Behind him, Al slunk into the room, retching and holding one hand over his mouth, talking around it fast and placatingly to the man who had just knocked half his teeth out:

"Charlie's honest-to-God right, boss." The words were slurred and slobbery in his eagerness to re-establish good will with Derr. "I swear she ripped that dress open herself to give us an eyeful. Lotsa these here society dames are like that," he went on sagely. "I recollect one that usta chase Fatso Golan 'round the room and try to grab—"

"Shut up," Derr said wearily over his shoulder. "Both you lame brains listen close. It was bad enough the way you messed this job by jumping the gun, but by God, if either one of you lays a finger on her while I'm gone, I'll fix you so you'll never do it again in all your lives. Get that?"

Charlie spat out the matchstick and said aggrievedly, "Hell, Boss. We was just thinkin'—"

Derr said coldly, "Don't wear out what's left of your brains by trying to think. This girl's worth plenty, and she's going to be delivered back home just like she was when you grabbed her." He paused thoughtfully. "Either of you ever hear the name Morgan Wayne?"

"Sure," Al said thickly from behind his palm. "Ginzo from out west, Chi or somewheres, they say's casing around to move in on the racket. Been nosing around getting leads and talking to some of the boys."

"From L.A.," said Charlie positively. "I got it straight from Peewee Lampell. He's a big shot out there, but with stuff getting tight from over the border, he figures on hornin' in here."

"No matter," said Hake Derr curtly, "where he's from or how he figures. He's already horned in just this much too far." He held his right hand up for both men to see, with thumb and forefinger widely extended. His round eyes seemed to protrude farther from the blandly boyish features and his voice became guttural as he stared directly in front of him at nothing and was pleased by the image his mind cast there.

"I'm headed for a messy kill," he said, and both men shrank away from the distilled vitriol that dripped from his thick lips. "You know what I mean. The way I like it." He paused and licked his lips and an anticipatory shudder traversed his heavy body. You didn't look at his boyish face now. You looked at his eyes and you heard his voice. "You boys wait for me here and keep the girl quiet till I get back. Lay one finger on her and you know what you'll get."

He turned away slowly and went toward the door. Al drew aside to let him go by. Both men were silent until they heard the front door slam shut. Then Al said in an awed voice, "It was the Gingham Gal, Charlie. She's fingered this Wayne character, sure as hell."

Charlie shrugged. He said, "Hake's been set to drink blood ever since we heard tell this Wayne creep was nosin' around." He looked down regretfully at the bound body of the girl on the bed and muttered, "Damn if I don't feel sorry for her right now. I swear she's been givin' me the come-on ever since we tossed her there." He stepped closer to the bed and cocked his head on one side. He pursed his thin lips and grinned down at her exposed breast.

"Hey!" said Al thickly. "You heard what Hake said if you laid a finger on her."

"But this won't be no finger," said Charlie.

Chapter Five

PRISCILLA ENDICOTT had assured Wayne it would take Hake Derr at least half an hour to reach the Gingham Gardens from the place where she had telephoned him. The address was on the East Side near the Triborough Bridge, and while he whipped northward on East River Drive, Wayne wondered grimly if that was just wishful thinking on Priscilla's part, because she wanted to believe Derr couldn't make it in time to interrupt whatever was going on in her bedroom. Or was it another point against her? A come-on to lure him into hanging around until Derr could bust in on them?

He didn't know. Not yet. Not until he found out for sure that she realized Derr was hearing her whispered conversation while she held the phone pressed against her body.

One thing Morgan Wayne did know for sure: It wasn't going to take his Cadillac more than twenty minutes to make the trip. He had no plan of action worked out. All that would have to depend on what he found when he reached the address. Letty Hendrixon might not even be there, of course. But he thought she would be. It was evidently some sort of hideout of Hake Derr's. Certainly not his regular place of residence. A man like Hake Derr wouldn't be caught dead living out that far from the center of things. When he was finally run to ground he would almost certainly be found ensconced in a swanky apartment on Central Park West or a similar neighborhood.

No. This address had the sound of a place from which some of his boys might reasonably operate, and Derr's presence there at this time argued that Letty had been taken there directly after being grabbed on the Sawmill

River Parkway—to be held, maybe, until dark before being transferred to safer quarters aboard the boat.

Why?

Because the boat wasn't ready to put out immediately. Wayne's unremitting and day-long vigils from the window of his office proved that. And they wouldn't risk bringing her aboard to be held for long while it was tied at the dock.

But why had they jumped the gun? Why hadn't they waited to grab the girl until the boat was provisioned and staffed for a quick getaway to safety on the open seas? They needed time for lengthy negotiations on a thing like this. It wasn't as simple as a one-night stand while a demand for ransom was made and payment swiftly arranged. This deal was much more delicate and complicated. There were difficult details to be worked out before the girl could be released.

And that brought up further questions—questions that had bothered Morgan Wayne for the last three weeks while he pursued various devious lines of inquiry into Hake Derr's background and current business affiliations.

Derr wasn't the man to have figured this sort of really big-time proposition. It wasn't in his line. Oh, sure, he was the sort to handle the details of the snatch, all right, and maybe was good enough for a cover-up in the final ransom negotiations, but there had to be someone much higher up who had planned this bold coup and who was in a position to profit by it once it was successfully concluded.

Which it wasn't going to be, Wayne told himself grimly as he gunned the Cadillac around a taxi that was only doing forty, nosed in through a crack in northbound traffic to hit a clear lane, and whipped up to seventy to slide past the next light just as it was turning against him.

Morgan Wayne's three weeks of vigilance had paid off this afternoon, even if Hendrixon, that stuffed shirt, had sneered at his warning a month ago and refused to take any action himself.

All in all, this snatch would make things a lot easier, Wayne reflected. It would throw the fear of God into Hendrixon, and by God, they'd have to listen to him now.

If he got the girl home safely. *When* he got her home safely, he corrected his thinking grimly as he put on another burst of speed and began looking for an exit from the Drive that would take him to the address in the shortest time. Every second counted now. Only God knew what sort of hoodlums Derr would leave in charge of the kidnaped girl while he beat it to the Gingham Gardens to confront the man he thought to catch fouling his nest.

That was bad. It would have been almost better if Derr had stayed around until Wayne arrived. He was a businessman, at least, playing for high stakes in this thing, and he'd take every precaution to see that the girl wasn't harmed. It might be different with his gorillas. Wayne had never met Letty, but he had seen pictures of her. Jail bait, of course, for any man who laid a finger on her, but a damned provocative girl. There was something about the overdeveloped lushness of her breasts that showed through in every picture Wayne had seen. That, and a short, pouting upper lip and a come-and-get-me-if-you-dare look in her eyes that would do things to the sort of hoods Derr would employ. She was the crazy sort of kid who might taunt them, Wayne told himself bitterly, braking hard and swinging on two wheels off the Drive, slowing now to search for street names and numbers.

Wrapped up in the inviolability of wealth, a youngster like Letty Hendrixon was completely unpredictable. She might even be getting a kick out of the whole thing. They got jaded early in life, these spoiled brats of New York society parents. Following the unhealthy examples of their elders.

No time for more thinking about that now. Here was

the street. The next block would be it. Get Letty Hendrixon out and then see what lengths she had driven the boys to.

Morgan Wayne slid past the intersection and slowed. It was a run-down neighborhood of long-ago elegance, one of those peculiar real-estate developments that mushroomed over a few connecting blocks in the Eighties when the city was rousing itself and stretching northward, when those small suburbs were as fashionable as Westchester is today.

The houses along this block on both sides were exactly uniform. Three-story brownstones, two rooms wide and two deep. Built with less than a foot of space between each one, with windows exactly similar and facing each other. A small porch in front with four stone steps leading up to a weathered front door that Wayne knew would open onto a tiny hallway with dining room on one side and living room on the other in front. A kitchen behind the dining room and library opposite. Four bedrooms and two baths on the second floor, servants' quarters above—for they had been built in the days when there were servants.

Wayne pulled past the number he sought and parked in front of the next house. He stepped out casually and glanced up to see a sleazy curtain drawn aside and a round-faced woman peering out at him and his Cad with unashamed curiosity.

He decided swiftly on a plan of action and went up the steps next door to the house in which he felt certain Letty Hendrixon was being held prisoner.

He didn't have to press the bell. The woman had seen him start up and was at the door before he reached it. She wore a dingy white cloth tied about her head and a faded cotton wrapper belted too tightly about her slovenly figure. Her eyes snapped with curiosity from between folds of fat, and Morgan Wayne knew his first impression had been right. If anyone in the block knew about the house next door and would be eager to share her knowledge with a well-dressed stranger, it would be this woman.

He smiled pleasantly and at the same time acted surprised to see her. "I'm looking for some friends of mine in this block. I thought the house was this number, but I I guess I'm mistaken."

"What name you want, mister? I know everybody in this block, 'cepting these new people next door."

"They must be the ones I'm looking for," Wayne said quickly. "When did they move in?"

"Just rented it a month ago." Her voice and face showed sour disapproval. "Not one bit neighborly, they ain't. Too uppity for others that live right next door. You mark my words, I told John just last night—that's my husband—you mark my words, I told him, them folks aren't up to no good. Coming and going all hours, with their fancy automobiles and fancier women. Not that folks ain't got a right to fancy automobiles," she went on grudgingly with a glance past Wayne at his convertible parked in front, "but when they think that makes 'em too good to pass the time of day with a body—"

"I know exactly what you mean," Wayne threw in hastily.

"And drinking and all that," she swept on, disregarding the interruption. "Staggerin' up the front steps right in broad daylight. It's a shame and disgrace to a decent neighborhood. I seen it with my own eyes not two hours ago—and her just a young girl, too. If they're friends of yours, mister, you can tell 'em plain out that we're decent folks here and don't want to have no truck with such doings."

Wayne said harshly, "They're not really friends of mine. I just told you that in the beginning to get a line on them. In fact, I came here looking for a young girl such as you describe, who I'm afraid is running around with them and learning to drink—and maybe worse," he added, dropping his voice. "An innocent girl, ma'am.

My own sister. If she's in that house now, I'm going in after her."

"Lord bless you for a good brother," said the fat woman. "She's in there, all right, with two of 'em. Another one drove away in his fancy car not more'n ten minutes ago."

Morgan Wayne's face became very grave, his voice somber. "If I could be sure it's Annie," he muttered, "I'd tear the place apart with my bare hands to rescue her. But they'll recognize me if I go to the door and they'll just deny she's there, and I don't want to call the police and have a lot of publicity if it is my sister."

"You poor soul," she breathed sympathetically. "Tell you what: I've been listenin' some to 'em moving around in there . . . you know, since seeing 'em bring her up the steps staggering drunk and wonderin' what was what. Well," she dropped her voice conspiratorily, "best I could tell from listening at the windows, they got her up in the front second-floor bedroom on this side. There's a window right opposite my bedroom window, but it's closed tight an' the shade's pulled and you can't see in, but if you listen close at my window you can hear voices maybe, and that way you'll know if it's her or not."

Wayne said, "That's a wonderful idea. If I just *knew* . . ." He pushed past the woman into a small unlit hallway that smelled dankly of boiling cabbage, and she wheezed after him happily, directing him in a hoarse whisper: "Up them stairs right straight ahead, mister. I'll come along and show you where."

Morgan Wayne sprinted up the stairs while she followed laboriously. He whirled into the front bedroom she had indicated and to an open side window with a rusty screen on it that was separated by less than a foot of space from a similar window in the adjoining house. It was closed, as she had said, and the shade was drawn, but Wayne did not hesitate for an instant. Too much time had already been wasted in working out this opportunity for paying a surprise visit. If Letty Hendrixon weren't the girl in the next bedroom . . .

He sprinted across the twilit bedroom, lowered his head, and, shielding his face with both arms, dove head-first through the two rusty screens and the glass of the other window.

He heard a faint scream behind him as he catapulted through the air and knew the hospitable fat woman was protesting his unorthodox exit, but her voice was immediately drowned by a crash of glass on the floor about him as his momentum carried him through the window and into the bedroom.

It was lighted by a dim ceiling bulb. Wayne slithered across the floor amid a clatter of glass and came to his feet in a half crouch as lightly as a cat, both hands diving into the side pockets of his jacket for the butts of short-barreled guns nested there.

In the single brief instant before the bedroom erupted into deadly violence, Wayne saw the naked and twisted limbs of a girl on the bed. Her face and torso were obscured from his view by the back and shoulders of a man on his knees beside the bed. Another man leaned over the foot of the bed looking down intently with sweat beading his forehead, a look of lascivious pleasure on his face despite smears of blood about his mouth and the absence of his upper front teeth.

For one instant of paralyzed shock, the tableau held its form. Then the kneeling man whirled with an inarticulate oath, and Al straightened up with a cry of fear.

Morgan Wayne coldly put a bullet in the center of his forehead before Al was fully erect. He crouched on the floor not two feet from Charlie's distorted face and slammed the solid weight of the smoking gun against the second man's jaw.

It made a solid clunk that shattered the jawbone, and Charlie's feral eyes glazed as his body slumped limply to the floor without a sound.

Through the smashed window Wayne heard the wailing shrill of the fat woman's voice raising the alarm, and knew he had only moments to get downstairs and away from the neighborhood.

He leaped to his feet and wasted only one glance at Letty's horror-stricken face, then swept her up roughly in his arms and tossed her over one shoulder like a bag of meal. He trotted out the door and down the stairs with her gagged mouth bouncing against his shoulder and one arm about her bare thighs in front of him.

Doors and windows were opening up and down the street and faint cries of question and alarm came through the twilight as Wayne raced to his parked car, but no one got in his way.

He tossed the gagged and trussed girl into the front seat and slid behind the wheel beside her, gunned the motor, and roared away to the first intersection without turning on the headlights. He made a screaming turn southward and continued two blocks without lights, slowed and turned right decorously and switched on his lights.

Only then did he relax and let out a deep breath and take his eyes from the road ahead to look down at the crumpled body of the girl he had rescued.

Her dress was still above her hips. The upper portion of her dress had been ripped wider, so that not only one full breast was completely exposed, but half of the other also. She lay twisted on the seat with her bound legs hanging over the edge, her head wedged against Wayne's hip and her eyes staring up at his face unblinking.

He reached over with one hand while driving at a moderate pace along the side street, jerked the handkerchief down over her jaw, and pulled the sponge gag from her mouth.

She moved her lips slowly, pressing them in and out against her teeth, but made no sound or other movement. Her eyes continued to stare unblinkingly upward at his face, filled with deadly fright and with something else that Morgan Wayne couldn't (or wouldn't) define. She hadn't moved a muscle, he thought, since he crashed into the bedroom back there and interrupted whatever was going on, and he wondered momentarily if the shock had completely paralyzed the girl.

Driving easily with one hand, he attempted to soothe and reassure her with a conversational tone. "It's all right now, kid. Take a deep breath and relax. I'll pull over in a shadowed place in a moment, and we'll cut you loose and straighten your clothes out. Don't you understand? It's all over. You're O.K. You can forget it ever happened."

Letty Hendrixon closed her eyes and spoke in a thin, little-girl voice that was wondering and awed and frightened, yet oddly and incredibly exultant.

"I don't want to forget it. I don't want it to be over. Why did you come so soon?" There was a plaintive and querulous note on the final words that caused Wayne to set his teeth together hard and summon all his will power to remain tactful and understanding.

"Listen to me, Letty. I'm a friend of your father's. Don't say those things. Don't think them. You've suffered a horrible shock, but you're all right. Don't forget that. You're *all right*." He emphasized the words harshly.

Directly ahead was a dark and vacant length of curbing with no curious strollers to take note of them. He eased in from the street and stopped. He turned and put both hands under the girl's shoulders to lift and turn her in the seat. She remained quiescent and limp, with closed eyes and lax mouth. He got a knife from his pocket and slashed the rope binding her hands, leaned down to unbuckle the belt about her legs.

She let him do as he would without helping or trying to help. She lay partly against the seat and partly against him, seemingly without the strength to open her eyes or hold her body erect. He slid his right arm about her shoulders, tugged the skirt down to her knees, and reached over with his left hand to draw the torn fabric of her dress together across her bosom, muttering, "If you've got a pin or anything . . ."

She didn't reply, but drew in a shuddering breath. One hand darted upward, thin fingers closing about Wayne's wrist in a grip of desperation and dragging his hand down across the full, bare breast while she moaned:

"He kissed it. Don't you understand? And I loved it. I almost died. I wanted him to go on and on. I burned all over." She was sobbing brokenly now, pressing her face down against Wayne's chest, clinging desperately to his wrist and trying to re-establish contact as he drew his hand away from the eager and pulsating flesh.

"Do you understand at all?" she sobbed. "Do you hear what I say? It seemed to be what I've always known I wanted—but didn't know." She stopped sobbing and she relaxed against Wayne. Her voice became dreamy.

"Do you know what I hoped he would do—what I think he would have done if you'd stayed away? Do other women feel as I do about it? Or is it just me? I don't care, do you hear?" She sat up defiantly and drew away from him, her voice becoming strident and far too mature for her years: "I loved it. I want it. I'll have it again."

Wayne's hand tightened on her shoulder and he shook her angrily. "You're hysterical. Get hold of yourself. For God's sake, forget what happened back there and get a grip on yourself."

"But I want to talk about it," she pleaded. "I want to know—"

"We'll talk about it later," he promised her through clenched teeth. "I'll tell you about Havelock Ellis and Kraft-Ebbing and give you some books to read. Right now, I've got to get you home to your parents. They must be frantic with worry about you."

"Nuts." Her tone changed again suddenly and she was like a schoolgirl. "Father probably doesn't even know I'm missing, and if Mother knows, *she* isn't worrying. She'll be far too busy with—well I'll tell you about that later. When we have a real talk about sex and stuff. Let's talk about it now." She snuggled down against him and caught his free hand again and ineffectually attempted to press it against her. "I've heard about Ellis and Kraft-Ebbing," she confided, "but no one ever let me get hold of them. Except a silly little abridged one-volume thing by Ellis that stopped and changed the subject whenever it began to get interesting. And I did get a look at the Kinsey Report, but I couldn't understand all the tables and graphs."

Wayne pulled his hand away from hers and asked sternly, "How old are you, Letty?"

"Almost seventeen. Plenty old enough to understand all about it, if people would just quit treating me like an infant. And plenty old enough to do it, too, I bet." She was rubbing her face against his shoulder ecstatically.

Wayne put his car in gear and began driving slowly toward the West Side Highway. His face was set and expressionless as he thought about the girl beside him. And then he thought about Priscilla Endicott and his foot went down on the accelerator hard and the heavy car leaped ahead. And about Lois Elling and the revealing letter she had idly typed in the office this afternoon, and the blood moved faster through his veins and his foot went harder on the accelerator.

Why was he wasting time here with this oversexed brat? Lois was waiting for him in her apartment.

"Well?" It was Letty's voice beside him, impatient and demanding. "Where are we headed in such a hurry?"

"Home," he said grimly. "Just as fast as we can get there."

"Good." She clapped her hands together excitedly. "I can't wait to get home with you and show you exactly—"

"To your home," he corrected her swiftly.

"But you promised to tell me all about . . ." Her voice quivered with rebellion and hurt.

"I promised to tell you sometime. When you grow up enough."

"Oh, no, you don't." She slid away from him to her side of the seat. "You turn right around and take me someplace where we can—well, talk, anyway."

"You're going home as fast as I can get you there."

"Then I'll scream," warned Letty tensely. "There's a police cruiser ahead. I'll scream bloody murder and say you kidnaped me."

"You'll keep your crazy mouth shut," growled Wayne. "My God, child, don't you realize—"

They were passing a slowly cruising police car. Letty leaned her head out the side of the convertible and screamed, "Help! Police! Help!"

The police cruiser came to life as Wayne cursed and grabbed her, pulled her down against him to smother her voice. The Cadillac leaped forward like a startled stallion and screamed through a red light. The lights of the police car faded momentarily and Morgan Wayne drove like one possessed, whipping around a bus and into the next intersection, skimming through another red light in the teeth of side traffic, with both hands on the wheel now and grimly alert while Letty sat beside him and laughed gaily as they grazed death by inches.

It was an absurd twist of fate, of course, but Wayne realized that danger from the police was desperately real. If a flash was out on the Hendrixon kidnaping—if either of the cruising cops had recognized her face as they flashed by—even if she had not been recognized, if they were alerted on the kidnaping, the chances were ten to one that the driver of a car with Letty as a passenger would never stay alive long enough to identify himself and explain the circumstances if the police cornered him with her.

Kidnaping is a hated and despicable crime, and official tempers run high if the victim is a young girl. He gave all his efforts to outdistancing immediate pursuit, and by twisting and speeding and breaking dozens of traffic regulations he eventually emerged on Madison Avenue in the Eighties, fairly certain that he had eluded that particular pursuer.

As he slowed to a moderate pace in a line of evening traffic, Letty glanced aside at him demurely, holding her torn dress together in front with one hand, and asked, "Where to now?"

"To my place," he told her angrily, "where I'm going to gag and hog-tie you and call your parents to come and get you. Don't you realize those cops got my license number and a description of this car and it's all over the city by radio already?"

"Of course," she said calmly. "Why else do you suppose I screamed at them?" She wrinkled her nose and smiled happily. "You'll see. When you start tying me up, I mean. Unless you're impotent. You're not, are you?"

Morgan Wayne groaned audibly and then shut himself into dour silence.

Chapter Six

Morgan Wayne was far from impotent, but right at the moment he wished fervently there were some way to convince Letty that he was. A lot of problems faced him and they all had to be solved fast, and her adolescent cravings weren't any help.

First and most important, he had to get his convertible off the street and securely out of sight. That was easily taken care of if he could make the next six blocks to his apartment hotel without being spotted. He could, he knew, get the use of another car easily enough from the hotel garage, where he was well known, and once that was accomplished it would be simple enough to drive Letty safely home if she were a normal girl and would consent to act normally. *If!*

Well, he realized by this time that she certainly wasn't a normal girl. But perhaps he could talk her into acting like one for just a little while.

Carefully tooling the car along the avenue in a discreet way so as not to attract notice, Wayne drew in a deep breath and began persuasively:

"No, Letty. I'm not impotent. But I am old enough to be your father and I've just killed a man and broken the jaw of another to rescue you from God knows what, and—"

"I've tried to tell you what," she reminded him breathlessly. "That is, maybe only God knows what really would have happened next if you hadn't come through the window the way you did, but I've got a pretty good idea, and you told me you had too back there, and you promised me . . ."

Wayne waited grimly until she ran out of breath and had to pause for an instant, and then broke in patiently:

"I'm trying to explain to you that this isn't the time or place for that. You've been *kidnaped,* goddamn it! There's probably a state-wide alarm out for you and anyone seen with you. Take it easy and let me get you home where you belong. After that will be time enough—"

"Oh, no, you don't," she broke in fiercely. "You don't put me off that way. For once in my life I've got a man in a spot where he can't run out on me when I start asking questions. You admit it yourself," she continued happily. "I'll only hold my dress together like this and go along with you quietly if you promise to take me up to your own place and—and forget you're old enough to be my father." She gave him a demure, sidelong glance and waited expectantly.

Wayne slowed carefully for a left-hand turn as he approached a red light. He was beginning to relax now. Another half block would do it. He said gently, "But I am old enough to be your father, Letty. Don't you see?"

"That's why I think I'm going to just love you to death," she told him ecstatically. "I'm tired to death of all the silly boys in my crowd who snatch a kiss in the dark and then get frightened and start apologizing because they don't know what to do next. You *will* know what to do next, I bet. And I don't mean just the conventional things, either."

Morgan Wayne sighed deeply and eased his car to the left in front of a line of traffic. He drove half a block to a marqueed, six-story structure of concrete and steel and swung across the sidewalk to a long ramp leading downward beneath the building with a sign overhead: "Hotel Patrons Only."

It was a large, well-lighted room with concrete floor and some thirty automobiles ranged about in private stalls. A uniformed attendant came sauntering over as Wayne pulled up in front of a small office and got out.

He said, "Evening, sir," very carefully keeping his gaze averted from the tousle-haired and thoroughly disreputable-appearing girl who was getting out on the other side.

His tactful disregard of Letty brought a slow smile to Morgan Wayne's lips and a five-dollar bill from his pocket. He said briskly, "Hello, Bill. I've been having some trouble with the ignition. Is there a good garage nearby that you could send it to tomorrow for a check-up?"

"Sure. The Ace Service on Lex. You won't be needing it, huh?" Still he did not glance at Letty, though she had opened the door and got out and was coming around the rear of the car toward them.

"As a matter of fact," said Wayne, "I will be needing a car, Bill. I'm going up for a while first," he went on hastily as he heard a swift indrawing of breath from Letty, "but I'll be going out later. Anything parked here I could use?" Another bill appeared between his fingers and then disappeared in the attendant's hand.

"Why, sure. There's a Hudson sedan over there in the corner. Belongs to a party that's out of town right now. No reason you shouldn't put a few miles on the speedometer. A careful driver like you."

"Swell." Wayne turned away as Letty sidled up to him and slid one arm through his. Without speaking, he led her toward the rear, where there was a small self-service elevator for the convenience of guests who wished to go directly up to their own rooms from the garage without going through the lobby.

And this was one time, Wayne thought to himself grimly, when he certainly didn't want to go through the lobby.

Letty held his arm tightly and didn't speak as he opened the door, followed her in and pushed the button marked 4. The grilled door slid shut smoothly.

Then she sighed and leaned against him and asked in a small voice, "Are you really angry with me for making you do this?"

Wayne bit his underlip to suppress a smile. He said, "Right now, I'm sore as hell, Letty."

"But you won't be for long." Her mood changed and she giggled happily, releasing the two torn pieces of dress she was holding together and letting her breast spill out for his approval. "You haven't even really *looked* at me yet. I'm not an infant. See?"

"I see too damned much," Wayne told her gruffly as the elevator stopped. "Pull that dress together while we go down the corridor. We might meet someone."

She giggled again and pulled the fabric together. Wayne opened the door and stepped out into a long, well-carpeted hallway. He went forward in long strides and Letty trotted happily after him, stopping by his side when he halted in front of a door and inserted a key. He reached inside to flip a switch that lighted four wall brackets to illuminate a square comfortable sitting room with deep chairs and smoking stands and a long sofa against one wall.

Letty pirouetted into the room ahead of him, making small sounds of excited pleasure, then stopped in consternation and dismay in front of a full-length mirror set in the closed door leading to the bathroom.

"Oh, my God!" she moaned, throwing both palms up to the sides of her disheveled hair dramatically and leaning forward to peer at her reflection in disbelief. "Why didn't you tell me I looked like hell before breakfast?" she wailed. "No *wonder* you don't think I've got any sex appeal."

Morgan Wayne closed the door on the night latch and strode grimly across the room to drop into a chair and reach for a cigarette in a silver box.

"How'd you think you looked after your bout with those hoodlums?" he demanded acidly. "Now that you've had a look at yourself, will you quit pestering me and agree to go home quietly?"

"But I'm still *me,*" she protested. "Underneath." She

dropped her hands from her hair to both sides of the torn bodice of her dress and deliberately ripped it down to the waist, then caught the top of her slip and tore it savagely, dragging the garments down and wriggling her slim body out of them until she stood in front of the long mirror wearing only low-heeled spectator pumps and stockings that drooped down about her slender ankles.

She stood with her back to him like that, regarding herself anxiously, and asked in a muffled voice, "See what I mean?"

"I do indeed," Wayne said. "You're top-heavy, my girl, that's what's the matter with you."

"I'm not either." She whirled about to face him angrily, cupping both hands beneath her heavy breasts. "See?" she challenged. "You're not looking at my mussed-up hair and my shiny nose now, are you?"

"No," Wayne told her moodily, "I'm not." He was looking at her, all right, but he was thinking about Lois Elling. What a hell of a note this was! How was he ever to convince this precociously nymphomaniacal little idiot that she was just wasting her time displaying her charms to him? She was crazy, of course. Absolutely blithering insane, with God knew what sorts of sexual repressions and frustrations. This afternoon had set her off, he realized. The ministrations she had received from Hake Derr's two hoods had turned the switch. He had been wondering how she had managed to stay out of an institution so long if she went around acting like this with every man she met, but now he realized it was probably the first time in her life she had ever let go.

The whole thing this afternoon had knocked her dizzy and she was still in a tailspin with excitement. Once back on the track, he told himself, once all this was behind her and she was safe amid familiar circumstances, she would probably be consumed with shame for the way she had acted.

But right now she was standing in front of him and he had to do something. It was a hair-trigger moment. God knew how she would react if he spurned her now. She was capable of anything—screaming for help and then swearing that it was he who had originally kidnaped her and brought her here for vile purposes of his own.

He crushed out his cigarette and got to his feet slowly. He hated himself for it, but his heart began to pound rapidly despite his resolutions as he approached her. Under other circumstances, goddamnit, he would give her the lessons she wanted and needed. So it wasn't so difficult to pretend and to make his voice sound husky with desire when he put his arms about her slim waist and felt the soft flesh beneath his palms quiver and the lush breasts pushing against him. He lowered his head as her mouth strained up to him, again hating himself fiercely for the surge of passion that went over him.

He muttered thickly, "All right, darling. You win. Go in there and take a fast shower and fix yourself up a little." He patted her shoulders and turned her about and opened the bathroom door and pushed her gently inside. She turned her head to look searchingly at him over a bare shoulder and he nodded reassuringly and said hoarsely, "Hurry it up. What do you think I'm made of?"

She said simply, "I'll hurry as fast as I can," and closed the door.

Morgan Wayne stepped back and let go a long withheld breath and dragged out a handkerchief to mop at the sweat streaming down his face.

He went swiftly to the telephone and dialed Julius Hendrixon's number. He got a busy signal and replaced the receiver. He stood for a moment with a frown, listening to the cheery swish of the shower from within the bathroom. It might be difficult to reach Hendrixon by telephone, he realized. After the kidnaping became known there would be all sorts of consultations and telephone calls, both incoming and outgoing. There would be police swarming all over the place. He became rigid suddenly, his face hardening to a mask of self-anger.

The police! Of course they'd be swarming all over the place, monitoring the phone calls, checking back on every incoming call before it was answered. They could arrange a busy signal easy enough. Right now his call was being traced. It would be only a matter of minutes before they knew where it had come from. Then a matter of seconds to alert the nearest precinct police and put a call on the radio for a cruising car in the vicinity.

What a fool he had been! That was the one thing he must avoid. If the police found him with the juvenile delinquent now making merry in his bathroom, there might easily enough be hell to pay. He had to get to the family first. Once his story was told, his position made clear, Letty could tell any damn-fool story she wished.

A matter of minutes was all he had. He moved swiftly and silently to the bathroom, grinned ruefully as he heard the shower still running. She was making a thorough job of her bath. Getting her young body all clean and fresh and fragrant for whatever sort of weird orgy her unhealthy mind anticipated.

He turned the outside lock slowly and carefully on the door so that it made no sound, whirled, and headed for the outer door. That would do it. He had complete faith in the efficiency of the New York police force. They would be here in a matter of minutes to discover her in the bathroom. Even before she tried the door and found she was locked in, perhaps. To make the job easier for them, Wayne left the outer door standing wide open as he went out and hurried back along the corridor to the elevator leading directly to the garage. He managed a grin and a chuckle as he envisioned the scene that would soon take place in his apartment. Grim-faced police officers entering cautiously and with drawn guns, finding her torn garments lying on the floor in front of the bathroom—and then the girl herself stepping out to confront them. . . .

He wondered fleetingly what sort of story Letty *would* tell the police. It didn't matter now. The only real danger to him since he had snatched her from Derr's mob had been the chance that some cop would find him with her and start shooting before Morgan Wayne could identify himself. He stepped out on the concrete floor of the basement garage and Bill nodded incuriously at him as he went across to the Hudson sedan that assured him safe transportation to Julius Hendrixon's house.

Chapter Seven

On this attempt, Morgan Wayne reached the West Side Highway without incident. It was dark now, and the heavy traffic was flowing in to the city instead of outward. Behind the wheel of the smoothly purring Hudson sedan, Wayne held himself to a careful sixty miles an hour in the outer lane, slowing decorously for first one toll bridge and then the next, then watching carefully for the Rontead Road exit, which he knew led directly to the Hendrixon estate, less than a quarter of a mile from the parkway.

He was relaxed behind the wheel, his thoughts racing as fast as the humming motor as he went back in retrospect over the events of the last few weeks, and particularly the bizarre happenings of the afternoon just past. All in all, he decided, things could be a lot worse. His information had proven correct, and Julius Hendrixon wouldn't be disposed to laugh at him now. It was probably the best thing in the world that the kidnaping had actually taken place as he had warned the drug tycoon it would. In a sense, Wayne's vigil in the improvised office overlooking the Flushing yacht basin had been wasted time because they hadn't brought the girl to the boat after all, but that was a minor detail. There had been no way of foreseeing that development.

Thoughts of the office and the long hours spent there, brought him up with a jolt to serious consideration of his latest in a series of secretaries making a one-week stand. Since hastily reading her "letter" to him late that afternoon, there hadn't actually been a single moment of respite for thoughts of Lois Elling and what he was going to do about her.

He grinned wryly in memory of the typed words as he

61

tooled the sedan smoothly along the winding four-lane highway. Had the other secretaries felt that way about him and about the job? If so, they hadn't shown their feelings. He frowned as he thought back over each of the three and tried to guess how they might have felt. It wasn't any good. He didn't really remember much about any one of them. Girls whom he had employed sight unseen from agencies to sit at a desk eight hours each day waiting for a telephone call. He hadn't paid any attention to them. He couldn't even recall what they looked like. A pretty colorless trio, they must have been, he thought. Not at all like Lois Elling.

Then he corrected himself. Maybe that wasn't fair to her predecessors. Until this afternoon he had scarcely noticed Lois, either. As a person. Right now, he couldn't recall any actual details of her features and coloring.

But her personality was something else. What Lois Elling *was* behind the veneer that civilized people put up between themselves and others.

Oh, yes. He knew all about Lois Elling now. As much, he thought, as a psychoanalyst after a year of treatments. And the hot fever of desire rose swiftly within his body as he reviewed all the things he knew about Lois Elling.

She must be waiting for him in her apartment now, damn it. Soaking up the warmth of a hot bath while she waited for him and anticipated his coming. He savagely cursed the circumstances that were keeping them apart, and unconsciously trod the accelerator closer and closer to the floor boards as he recalled the words she had typed while sitting not more than ten feet from him only a few hours ago.

A man would know where he stood with Lois Elling. There'd be no artifices or sham. She would be as straightforward and honest about sex as a man. There would be no fumbling between them. No false modesty or silly attempt to hide from the truth.

In that sense, there was a strong similarity between

Lois and the Gingham Girl. The way Priscilla had first looked at him across the room. The flame that had been ignited and which they both recognized and accepted as he moved toward her. A man knew where he was with Priscilla Endicott, too.

Or did he? Either she was blatantly honest or else she was one of the most devious and dangerous females he had ever encountered. He wanted desperately to believe that her phone call to Hake Derr had been on the level—that she had no idea Derr would hear her whispered aside to Wayne while she waited. He wanted desperately to believe that the flame lighting the translucent depths of her green eyes had been honest passion of such intensity that it could not be denied.

But he couldn't be sure. Not yet. But he would be sure. And soon, he promised himself. After this night with Lois Elling he'd be in just the sort of shape to take Priscilla's lovely white body in his two hands and tear the truth out of her.

Right now there were other things to think about. The coming interview with Hendrixon was all-important. Every sense was alert as he saw the exit sign in front of him and slowed for the turn. A state police car was discreetly parked on the grass at the exit where the two troopers could look over any car that turned from or sought to enter the parkway at this point. Wayne gave them a levelly incurious glance as he drove past in his borrowed Hudson and they made no move to stop or follow him.

That was only the beginning of the police gantlet he would have to run before reaching Hendrixon, he knew, and he drove along the macadam slowly, prepared for the signal that didn't come until the gravel turnoff leading upward to the baronial structure he sought.

There was a businesslike roadblock here. A county police car and another state cruiser with two smartly uniformed troopers. One of the troopers and a man in plain

clothes stood side by side in the driveway with flashlights
that blinked on and off. Wayne rolled up to them and
they separated to let him stop opposite them. The trooper
leaned against the door on Wayne's left and casually
flashed his light over the back seat, then brought it to
bear on Wayne's face. "Mind giving us your name and
business, mister?"

Morgan Wayne said, "Not at all," with a smile. His
right hand was ready in his trousers pocket and he
brought it out with a small gold medallion cupped in the
palm. He held it for the flashlight beam to bring out the
inscribed words and waited patiently while the trooper
studied it with care.

The man pushed his broad-brimmed hat back from his
forehead and studied the driver with interest and respect.
"I've heard of those do-jiggers," he drawled, "but this is
the first time I ever had one flashed on me. You're Morgan
Wayne?"

Wayne said, "If you want further indentification . . ."
His hand moved upward toward his inner coat pocket,
but the trooper said hastily, "That'll be O.K. Straight
up the drive and park behind the other cars so there's
room to get by." He stepped back and fingers went up to
touch the brim of his hat in a salute.

Wayne said, "Thanks, Officer," and drove on in second gear up the steep grade to the huge hilltop mansion
that spilled light from every window.

There were at least a dozen cars parked bumper to
bumper in the wide circle in front of the house. Wayne
slide in behind the last one and got out to make his way
past half a dozen of them, noting that every degree of of-
ficialdom seemed to be represented, from a parkway
police car to a sleek blue sedan with modest insignia in-
dicating a high official in the New York Police Department.

He turned under a porte-cochere and went up a wide
flagstoned walk protected by an awning to the front

doors, which stood open. Another state trooper stood there beside a cadaverous butler in a black suit with a stiff wing collar and string tie about his gaunt neck. The trooper was young and personable. He stepped in front of Wayne negligently and inquired, "Whom do you wish to see?"

"Mr. Julius Hendrixon. Tell him Morgan Wayne," he said past the trooper to the butler.

The trooper's face showed interest and he nodded. "Mr. Hendrixon has given orders to admit you. Take Mr. Wayne into the small library, Dillon," he added to the butler.

Wayne followed the black-clad figure down a wide hallway with rosewood paneling to double sliding doors that stood partially open. He entered and announced, "Mr. Morgan Wayne," and stood aside for Wayne to enter.

The "small" library was a room some sixty by forty feet, with quartered oak flooring and a fieldstone fireplace at the far end large enough to have roasted a yearling whole.

Both side walls were solid bookshelves from floor to ceiling, and there were heavy tables and leather chairs scattered about. Four persons stood in a group near the center of the room and turned their heads to look at Wayne as he entered. He recognized only one of them.

With his heavy body, shaggy mane of dark hair, and a last-generation British mustache, Julius Hendrixon had something of the look of a water buffalo. His heavy features might have been hewn from granite by an inexpert hand, and the heavy torso was hunched forward a trifle as though almost too heavy for the bowed legs beneath.

He swung away from the others and advanced toward Wayne, booming aggressively. "Wayne! I've been wondering, by God, where you were. It's no good now, you see. We just had a flash from New York that Letty has been found by the police. Unharmed."

Wayne said, "That's very good news." He didn't voice his fears for the safety of the police detail who had found her. "Better than you deserve," he went on dryly, "after the way you shrugged off my warning of this very thing last month."

"I admit my mistake." Hendrixon's voice lost some of its booming aggressiveness and became shaken and worried. "And that's what I want to talk to you about now. How you knew it was planned. Why you refused to give me any credentials or proof."

"And how, Mr. Wayne," came a cold voice from behind him, "you were aware of the fact practically as soon as it happened."

"That's right," Hendrixon put in heavily. "The call from your secretary came before we were aware that Letty was gone."

Wayne made a gesture of dismissal and said shortly, "I've had a man on Miss Hendrixon day and night ever since you gave me the brush-off in your office. He witnessed the snatch this afternoon and phoned me at once." He moved forward past Hendrixon toward the other three people in the room, a woman and two men.

The woman was tall and thin, modishly gowned and about forty. Letty's mother, Wayne knew at a glance, though this anemic socialite with her thin lips and haughty manner and high hair-do was a far cry from the impetuously carnal youngster he had left in his bathroom. A vague memory of something Letty had said or implied about her mother tugged at his mind as he neared the trio. He studied her through low-lidded eyes as he approached and decided he had misunderstood Letty. Certainly this sterile product of an unhealthy, hothouse environment had never known an honest emotion in her life.

He jerked his thoughts back to more pressing matters as he looked the men over coldly. One was young and foppish in a velvet-lapeled fawn-colored smoking jacket, pleated slacks, and patent-leather pumps, with a weak face that had the double disadvantage of a receding chin and protruding upper teeth. The other man was middle aged and ruddy faced, wearing a conservative business suit and chewing on half of a dead Perfecto.

Behind Wayne, Hendrixon said, "This is Letty's mother, who has asked to meet you, Wayne. And her brother, John Durtol Third."

He paused momentarily and the young man said limply, "I've been telling Julius that all this furor is utterly absurd. I'm convinced this so-called kidnaping was engineered by Letty herself just to get what she would call a thrill. You see, I know something about my charming niece's proclivity toward—"

"John!" Wayne was mildly surprised by the vehemence of the thin, high voice that came from Mrs. Hendrixon's lips. One would not have guessed such spirit lay hidden behind that cold exterior. "We'll listen to no more of your filthy insinuations about Letty," she continued almost breathlessly.

He shrugged elaborately and moved aside to sprawl in a big leather chair and stare at the polished tips of his shoes.

"I'm Elliot Carson," said the big, ruddy-faced man, extending a fleshy palm and gripping Wayne's hand firmly. "Attorney for the Hendrixon estate," he added. "Blair, Carson, and Withers. This may not be exactly the time for a full explanation from you, Mr. Wayne, but I assure you that I am prepared to take any necessary legal measures to force you to divulge the sources of the information you offered Mr. Hendrixon a month ago."

Wayne shrugged his broad shoulders and said blandly, "And I assure you, sir, that any legal steps you may take will be utterly wasted. You fools!" he went on angrily. "Standing around here driveling about legal measures when you didn't even have brains enough to protect a young girl from what Letty went through this afternoon."

"Just what did dear Letty go through this afternoon?" drawled John Durtol Third insolently from his leather chair.

"And how much do you know about the details?" demanded Hendrixon. "Do you realize your phone message is the only one we've received concerning her?" One huge fist thumped resoundingly into a meaty palm. "No demand for ransom. No nothing. I'm prepared to swear out a warrant—"

Wayne interrupted him harshly. "What you had better do is start listening to me instead. This thing has just started, and God knows where it may end. It may not be Letty next time, but it'll be something else."

He was looking into Mrs. Hendrixon's cold eyes as he spoke, and he sensed an inexplicable change in them. Not a warmth, for he felt it impossible for them to show that, but a flicker of interest or of excitement. An almost avid awakening as though something within her responded to his harshness.

"To hell with this," Wayne said abruptly. He turned to the lawyer. "Who is the highest police officer in the house?"

"Inspector Hibbs from Manhattan. He drove out with me as a personal favor."

"Will his O.K. satisfy you as to my integrity?" Wayne demanded with savage force.

"Why . . . yes. Certainly. If you can convince the inspector . . ."

"Take me to him," Wayne said

As he turned to move away with Carson, his gaze touched Mrs. Hendrixon's again. She was wetting her thin lips with the tip of her tongue and her nostrils were flared at the base. There was a peculiar intensity about her staring eyes that gave Wayne a momentary queasy feeling at the pit of his stomach. He followed Carson out into the hallway again, striving to recall what Letty had said about her mother.

Carson went toward the rear a short distance and entered a smaller room with half a dozen men lounging about with drinks. He spoke to a tall, aquiline-nosed man wearing shaggy tweeds and with a highball glass in his hand. "Inspector Hibbs."

The Inspector came to the doorway looking at Wayne inquiringly.

"This man," began Carson portentously, but Wayne cut him short:

"Let me handle this, please." And to the Inspector, "Will you step aside with me a moment, sir?"

The inspector stepped into the hallway with him and Wayne said urgently, "These people are in the middle of one hell of a spot, and they're wasting time quibbling about whether I can be trusted or not. Carson has agreed to take your word about that." As he spoke he again removed the gold medallion from his pocket and let the inspector see it. Unlike the state trooper below, the veteran policeman needed only a glance before saying heartily, "Certainly. Happy to accommodate you."

Wayne said, "Thanks." He drew back and allowed the inspector to rejoin Carson and speak to him briefly, after which the attorney hurried forward and admitted cordially, "He says you can be trusted to the limit. No offense taken, I trust. There are certain precautions . . ."

"That's all right," Wayne said shortly. "Let's go back to the others and—"

There was a commotion down at the end of the long hall in front of them. Two uniformed officers led a giggling Letty between them, barefooted and wearing Morgan Wayne's best brocaded dressing gown wrapped tightly about her body.

Chapter Eight

CARSON hurried forward with an exclamation of pleasure as the girl was ushered into the room where her parents and uncle awaited her. Wayne followed more slowly. He hadn't the slightest idea what sort of wild story Letty had told the cops when they discovered her alone in his apartment. The apartment was rented under a different name and no one in the building knew him as Morgan Wayne, so there was no way the police could connect the two—unless Letty put the finger on him now.

He frowned thoughtfully as he strolled forward, planning how to handle it if she did start singing the moment he entered the room. And she probably would, he thought ruefully. Just to strike back at him for locking her in the bathroom and leaving her there to be found by the cops.

Well, he'd have to take it in his stride, he decided. Tell the whole thing just as it had happened. He didn't want to. He didn't want to bring Hake Derr and the Gingham Girl into it. Not yet. That was his private angle. There was some person high above Derr who was ramrodding this whole affair, he was certain. And so long as Wayne could keep his knowledge of Derr a secret, he would have an inside track in ferreting out the identity of the man who really counted.

He paused in the corridor just outside the open double doors, got out a cigarette, lit it meditatively, and leaned forward for a quick look inside the room.

The two New York officers who had returned the girl to her family were standing together near the doorway, looking on at the reunion and grinning furtively at each other while they listened to Letty's breathlessly babbled and highly colored account of her kidnapping and rescue.

Her mother was seated in a chair and Letty was perched on the arm of it, hugging Wayne's dressing gown tightly about her with one hand while the other was clasped tightly between her father's palms as he bent over her in an attitude of affectionate concern. Carson stood back a few feet listening to her story with interest, while her youthful and vapid-faced uncle sat across from her and listened with patent disbelief.

"They were just the most awful hoodlums," Letty was saying rapidly when Wayne came in on the story. "They tied me up tight and put a gag in my mouth and said the most awful things about what they were going to do to me, and I guess there must have been ether on the gag or something because I just passed right out there in the car and didn't know another single thing until I came to in that apartment and there was this other man alone with me."

She paused dramatically, licking her lips while she fashioned the next segment of her story together, and Wayne nodded with mute approval. That was O.K. That was fine. She was taking exactly the line he would have asked her to take. This was leaving Hake Derr and Al and Charlie out of it altogether. If she kept it up that way there would be nothing whatever to connect either her or Morgan Wayne with the occupants of the brownstone house when the dead gangster's body was found there beside his companion with the shattered jawbone.

Wayne stayed in the corridor out of the girl's sight and listened with amusement to Letty's free-wheeling and imaginative recapitulation of her imprisonment in the apartment where she had been found.

"He was . . . I just don't know how to describe him," the girl went on with a shudder. "I've told those two policemen about him already." She looked toward the pair standing together near her, and one of them nodded.

"We've got a good description of the man. Marcus Knowlton, he calls himself. He's been in that place two months and no one knows much about him. Laying low from some other rap, most likely. Planning this snatch down to the last detail."

"But *why*?" exclaimed Hendrixon. "Why my daughter? What did he want from her?"

"Now, Daddy," said Letty quickly and reprovingly. "I hate to tell this right out in the open, but if you force me to, I will. I did have to tell the officers already," she conceded, looking so naïve and frightened that Wayne had to choke back his laughter.

"He's crazy, of course," she went on complacently. "A sexual maniac. But in a nice but awfully peculiar way," she went on swiftly, wrinkling up her nose in a little-girl frown as though she were striving to be completely fair, "You wouldn't think it to see him at all. He was really nice. Big and broad-shouldered, but grim, sort of. He apologized right off," she hurried on glibly, "for using force that way to get me in his clutches, but swore he just couldn't help himself. He's been clipping my pictures out of the newspapers, you see, and fallen madly in love with me."

This time John Durtol III did laugh out loud when Letty paused. He sank back in his chair choking with mirth and waved one thin hand in the air. "Honestly, Let! Of all the ridiculous adolescent—"

"John!" Mrs. Hendrixon sat erect and glared at her brother. "After all this child has been through! If you haven't the decency to be quiet and listen to her, you'd better leave the room."

"Oh, no. My God, I wouldn't miss this show for a million dollars. Go right ahead, Let," he urged. "Tell us what the big bad man wanted from you so much that he arranged a kidnaping to get it."

"You needn't laugh about it!" exclaimed Letty indignantly. "It was simply terrible when I realized he was a maniac and had me there alone with him where he could do what he wanted with me." She sat erect on the arm of her mother's chair and leaned forward so the lapels of the dressing gown fell open and showed bare flesh beneath.

"You just ask the officers what they found when they broke in and rescued me. Every stitch of my clothes torn off me, that's what. And locked in the bathroom." She caught her underlip beneath her teeth and shook her head slowly as if all this was simply too much for a simple child like herself to comprehend.

"He talked awfully funny," she confided to them all. "About people named Havelock Ellis and Mr. Kraft and Mr. Ebbing. And—and it was all so strange and indecent that I just don't want to talk about it any more."

From his point of vantage in the corridor, Wayne had a clear view of Mrs. Hendrixon's face while Letty spoke. The thin nostrils were widely flared again, and the haughtily patrician features seemed to contract and tighten. There was again the queer flicker in the depths of the cold eyes, somehow repellent and evil.

"Oh, really now, Let!" The girl's uncle was rocking back and forth in his chair with laughter. "So this character out of Kraft-Ebbing stripped you down . . ."

"I won't have you laughing at me!" shrilled Letty. She leaped up from the arm of her mother's chair and fled toward the doorway into the corridor. Mrs. Hendrixon rose hastily to follow her with a withering look and an angry exclamation for her younger brother, and Wayne stepped back two paces, thrust out a long arm to intercept the girl as she dashed through the doorway.

Letty squealed with surprise when his arm circled her waist, then she drew back with a hissing intake of breath when she saw his face.

"You were marvelous in there," he told her swiftly and emphatically. "Don't blame me for running out on you. I had to. I knew the police were coming and we'd *never* have a chance to be alone together if they found me. As it is now . . . if they don't suspect . . ."

"We *will* be alone together?" she interrupted happily. "Promise? Cross your heart and hope to die?"

"I promise," he whispered fiercely. "Just don't tell anyone." He slid his arm from about her waist and took firm hold of her wrist as Mrs. Hendrixon appeared beside them and continued in a conversational tone, ". . . realize you're upset now, and I want to talk to you about that man again. I think I may know something—"

He broke off as though in surprise at her mother's presence and told her smoothly, "I overheard a portion of your daughter's story, Mrs. Hendrixon, and detained her to ask for a meeting later when she's less upset. I think it's quite possible," he went on deliberately, "that I may be able to locate the man who calls himself Marcus Knowlton, with your daughter's co-operation."

"I see." Mrs. Hendrixon's coldly suspicious gaze moved slowly from Letty's flushed cheeks and heaving bosom to Wayne's imperturbable face. "Who are you, Morgan Wayne?" she asked, spacing the words carefully. "I'm afraid I don't understand your position in all this."

"Yes," echoed Letty uncertainly. "Who are you? I never saw you before, did I?"

Wayne had no idea how well or poorly that got over to Mrs. Hendrixon. She was watching him fixedly, waiting for a reply to her question.

"Did Carson tell you that Inspector Hibbs vouches for me?" demanded Wayne.

She said, "Yes. He told us. But I understand now that you warned my husband a month ago that Letty was in danger. From a sexual maniac?" There was a touch of cold scorn in her voice.

"Hardly, Mrs. Hendrixon." Wayne matched her tone with a curt flatness of his own that was like flint striking steel. "I'm inclined to think that perhaps your daughter —ah—misinterpreted the motives of her kidnaper."

"You listen here," began Letty violently, but neither of the older persons paid the slightest heed to her. Their eyes were locked together in a sort of duel of wills, mutual antagonism flaring swiftly between them. The woman's eyes narrowed and her lips thinned out against sharp teeth. There was something almost venomous in her silent appraisal, yet with it Wayne detected a surging undercurrent of seething emotion that repelled yet fascinated him.

The tableau held for a matter of seconds while Letty stood aside and watched them in helpless bewilderment, then Mrs. Hendrixon shook her head as though to break the spell and turned to Letty, saying shortly, "You must come again, Mr. Wayne, when Letty is more herself. I . . ." She hesitated and appeared to struggle to form the words. "I should like to see you also." She was moving away with Letty as she spoke the words and they came out jerkily.

Morgan Wayne stood very still for a moment and gazed after the mother and daughter speculatively. A session with Letty and then with her mother. That would be a day!

He shrugged and went inside the library to find Julius and his attorney eagerly questioning the two policemen about the details of Letty's rescue.

". . . locked her naked in the bathroom and tried to phone out here, it looks like," one of them was explaining, looking down at the toes of his shoes and speaking heavily. Wayne repressed a grin as he moved closer to the quartet. The poor cop was certainly on the spot, confronted by Letty's father and trying to explain the girl to him. Knowing Letty, Wayne had a pretty good idea what she would have said to the policemen when they opened the bathroom door and she saw them instead of the man she expected. But you couldn't tell that to a girl's father. Not if you were an ordinary cop and he was Julius Hendrixon.

Wayne stepped into the breach and interposed smoothly, "I spoke to your daughter in the hall just now, Hendrixon, and I doubt whether these officers can tell you as much about all this as I can. Hadn't you better let them report back while we have a brief talk?"

"I think it's damned well time you and I did have a talk," fumed Hendrixon. His hand went into his coat pocket for a wallet, and he turned to the two uniformed men.

"See here, I'm really grateful for your excellent work. Please let me express my gratitude a little more concretely." He was extracting bills as he spoke, but both men drew back stiffly and shook their heads and mumbled something about only doing their duty, and turned and hurried away as though happy to wash their hands of the whole affair.

Looking somewhat nonplused, Hendrixon turned away from them and boomed, "Now let's hear something that makes sense, Wayne. Carson here says the inspector gives you a clean bill of health. But who are you? What's your position in this matter? What is behind all this?"

Morgan Wayne shrugged and carefully lit a cigarette. He flipped the matchstick away onto the oak floor and lifted his eyebrows at the younger man slumped in his chair. He said, "This actually concerns Durtol Drugs, Incorporated. Is he in on it?"

Durtol blinked his eyelids at Wayne and said languidly, "I'm merely president of Durtol, that's all. How does this hocus-pocus with Letty concern the firm?"

Wayne frowned and told Hendrixon, "There must be some mistake. I understood you ran the corporation."

"John is the titular head," said Carson hastily. "Julius is chairman of the board and actually business manager."

Wayne said, "I see." He hesitated and then asked carefully, "Is it true that eighty per cent of Durtol stock is controlled by you, Hendrixon?"

"It is not," the young man snapped. "Actually, Julius doesn't own a single share. I own forty per cent and my sister, Julius' wife, owns a second forty per cent. The remainder is held in small blocks by outside parties."

Wayne nodded slowly, weighing this information for what it might be worth. "In effect, then," he said, "either you or your sister, by getting proxies from eleven per cent of the other stockholders, could control the affairs of the corporation?"

"That's theoretically true," boomed Hendrixon, "but hardly to the point. John and my wife have been perfectly satisfied thus far to take my advice on all matters connected with the business."

"Also," put in Carson smoothly, "the other twenty per cent of the stock is scattered quite widely in very small blocks and the owners are well content with the present management and the large dividends that are issued each year. I daresay it would be almost physically impossible to trace down enough small shareholders to constitute eleven per cent."

A trace of a smile flickered across Wayne's face. He directed himself bluntly to Hendrixon. "Do you recall that I warned you a month ago that someone seemed bent on doing exactly that? That small stockholders were being approached with absurdly high offers for their shares?"

"I do recall some such statement. But it was absurd on the face of it. Even if someone *did* wish to buy in heavily, what possible harm would it do? We still control the eighty per cent."

Wayne sighed. "And you mean to say neither your wife nor your brother-in-law has been approached recently with an offer to buy their shares at well above the market price?"

Hendrixon snorted and made a contemptuous motion of dismissal. "Perhaps they have. I can't speak for John. But a sale would be out of the question. My wife's grandfather founded the firm, beginning in a tiny laboratory in his own kitchen, where he evolved many of the formulas that are still big sellers in the drug field. Durtol Drugs is a family thing. It was expanded by the founder's son, and passed on as a sacred trust to *his* son and daughter in equal shares. It is inconceivable that either would sell out for any price."

Wayne sighed again. "Exactly, my friends. And that is why Letty was kidnaped."

The three men looked equally incredulous, Wayne noted as he glanced from one to the other, though the attorney appeared to grasp his meaning first. "You mean as a means to apply pressure? To force a sale of some of the Durtol stock?"

"To force the sale of forty per cent of it," said Wayne flatly. "Perhaps you'll begin to believe me if you'll make a study of the records of stock transactions during the past two months. You'll discover that more than one half of the outstanding stock has changed hands during that period. Quite a sudden flurry when you consider that before two months ago not a single share of Durtol stock had been sold for several years."

"Who is buying it up?" demanded Carson.

"It's being done cleverly by various agents who cannot be traced to a common source. I can't prove one man is behind it, you understand, but the facts speak for themselves. If you insist on closing your eyes to the obvious, I'm afraid I can't help you."

"The obvious being," said Carson slowly, "that someone has gathered up enough outstanding stock to gain control of the corporation if one of the blocks of Durtol stock were added to his present holdings."

"Exactly. And I knew a month ago that absurdly high offers had been refused for the Durtol stock. That's why I came to you with my warning," he reminded Hendrixon. "I don't know the *man* behind this, but I do know the vicious elements involved. They are openly out to get Durtol Drugs. They'll stop at nothing. Kidnaping Letty was the first and most obvious step. Next time it will be something else. Tomorrow perhaps. Or the next day.

They'll have to move fast now that they've come into the open."

"But why?" demanded Hendrixon, mopping his craggy face. "Durtol is a small and honorable firm. We're not big business like McKesson and Robbins, for instance. I understand things like this do go on when millions are at stake, but our net profit is less than a hundred thousand annually."

"It's because you *are* a small firm with a long and honorable reputation that you are the target," said Morgan Wayne grimly. "Durtol is exactly what they need for a front. If you haven't realized what I'm getting at yet, you're a trio of fools," he went on. "You say your net profits are less than a hundred thousand. What do you suppose they would amount to if your firm turned, say, twenty per cent of the morphine and similar drugs you use in legitimate manufacturing processes each year into illegitimate channels? Think it over a moment. As business manager, you should have a rough idea, Hendrixon. Keep in mind the findings of the Kefauver Committee that there's something like a thousand-per-cent profit between the legitimate wholesale price of heroin and the sum paid by the consumer. Is that enough motive?"

"But how could they accomplish much even if they did get control?" protested young Durtol. "We'd still go on as before, and—"

"On the surface, Durtol Drugs would still go on as before," agreed Wayne. "But don't you see what control would do? In the first place, there'd be a new chairman of the board—a new business manager, unless Hendrixon is a fool who could be used by them or a knave who would go along. Then changes in personnel all along the line. Old and trusted employees disappearing from the scene and new ones coming in to key positions."

"It's unbelievable," protested the attorney in a shocked tone. "This is 1952, Wayne. Such things aren't possible in a modern world."

"Such things *are* happening in the modern world and all about you," snapped Wayne. "Do any of you ever read a newspaper? Entire police departments corrupted and purchased by racketeers. City governments and even large segments of the federal government honeycombed with crooks and thieves. It's people like you who allow such things to happen by closing your eyes and blinding yourselves to the truth. Read the Kefauver report, for God's sake. Get some idea of the nastiness and horror that are creeping up on this country of ours. Unbelievable, hell! It's part of the pattern."

He thrust both hands deep into his pockets and looked from one face to another of the three men before him. After a moment, he said in a quiet voice:

"I killed a man this afternoon. I liked killing him. Think that over, gentlemen. And think over what I've told you. I'll be in touch with you tomorrow." He turned as though to go, but Hendrixon put out a hand to stop him.

"You . . . killed a man?" His heavy face expressed horror and distrust. "Once more, I demand to know: Who are you? How do you fit in this? How do we know we can trust you?"

Wayne smiled bleakly. "You don't, do you?" He shrugged off the other's restraining hand and started out, tossing over his shoulder, "I hope you'll pay some attention to *this* warning before it's too late."

"Warning of *what*?" The voice of John Durtol III was high-pitched and panicky. "Having failed in the kidnaping, what can they possibly try next?"

Morgan Wayne stopped in the doorway and shrugged. He said over his shoulder, "If you and your sister remain stubborn about not selling, if I were you I'd begin thinking about who will inherit your blocks of stock after your death. If either of you have heirs who might not be so scrupulous . . ." He paused to shrug again. "Well, if I were an insurance man I'd hesitate to issue a policy on either of your lives. And now," he went on easily, "I really must go. I have a date with a charming young lady who will be getting quite impatient, I'm afraid."

There was silence in the library behind him as he turned down the corridor to the outer door.

Chapter Nine

IT was characteristic of Morgan Wayne that he pushed every other thought out of his mind when he left the Hendrixon house behind him and headed toward the parkway and his date with Lois Elling. In more than thirty years of living, Wayne had learned a great many lessons, not the least important of which was that it behooves a man to appreciate any gifts of love offered by the capricious gods and to make as much of each such gift as is humanly possible.

He was wild with impatience now to see Lois. It seemed eons since the moment he had stood beside her typewriter reading the words typed by her hands and feeling an answering surge of emotion to her passion-ridden words that was equal to anything he had experienced before.

His brief encounter with Priscilla Endicott and with Letty had done nothing to make Lois seem less desirable. On the contrary, they had added fuel to his fierce wanting by arousing him to unsatisfied heights and by providing him with a basis for comparison from which Lois emerged as definitely more appealing.

She was a woman a man could talk to, he told himself, as he hit the parkway without seeing any officers and headed toward the city. A woman, by God, whom a man could listen to while lying beside her in the darkness and not be bored. Long ago, Morgan Wayne had learned how important this was to his real enjoyment of any romantic adventure. The only really worth-while experiences, those that were unforgettable and unregretted, were with women who were his intellectual equals and as charming companions at the breakfast table as in bed. A mingling of the minds as well as a fusing of the bodies, a condition of mental as well as physical rapport.

Although Wayne had met many men who denied similar feelings, he shrewdly suspected that the vast majority
of men felt much as he did. Witness the famous courte-
sans of the ages who had not only attracted the leaders of
their day by their physical charms, but had held them
bound in happiness and affection for years on end. No
mere sexy strumpets, they, but women of intellect and
sophistication. That's what holds men after the first wild
fervor is exhausted, and as he drove along swiftly Wayne
allowed himself to hope that was what he would discover
this night with Lois Elling.

Cold sweat stood on his forehead and his foot went
down heavily on the throttle as he thought about what
she had written. He grimaced and laughed shakily at himself and lifted his foot when he noticed the speedometer
needle flickering past eighty. Getting picked up on the
parkway for speeding wasn't the way to reach Lois fast.
Besides, he was acting like a callow young fool. Sure, he
was late. Probably much later than Lois had anticipated,
but she would wait. She knew he was coming tonight.
Those other nights, she had known he wasn't coming.

But he made no effort to turn his thoughts away from
Lois. He concentrated fiercely on visualizing her as she
must be waiting for him now. That was the only draw-
back to this affair. There hadn't been enough build-up.
Not enough expectation. Nothing at all of the slow and
delicious burning that gradually takes complete possession of a man during the period of delightful dalliance
that generally precedes the consummation of a civilized
love affair. He had to make up for that lack during this
brief period while he hurtled through the night toward
Lois' apartment.

Then he realized suddenly that he didn't even know
where her apartment was located. He assumed it was in
Manhattan, and fervently prayed that it was as he slowed
at the last toll gate to pass over his dime and then speed
on toward the blaze of city lights ahead. There was a gas

station ahead, and if the Manhattan phone book didn't yield her address he would be in one hell of a mess, he told himself disgustedly. Lord, he couldn't even go back to his own apartment tonight. Not that he wanted to or intended to, of course, not if he found Lois. But if he had to search for her name through all the other borough directories . . .

He slowed for the filling station, pulled in, and glanced at the gas gauge on the Hudson. It showed less than a quarter full, so he stopped at a pump and told the attendant to fill the tank with high test. Then he hurried inside to the telephone booths, flipped open the directory, and ran his gaze down the E's.

It was there. Elling, Lois. A West End Avenue address. He sighed with relief and was tempted for a moment to step into the booth and phone her.

He rejected the temptation and trotted back to the Hudson instead. He would be there in ten minutes. It wouldn't do to phone ahead now. It would sound like an apology for his lateness, or as though he questioned whether she would have waited for him so long.

He had no apology to make, and no real question about her being there when he arrived. She would understand that he had come to her as swiftly as was humanly possible. Without any explanations, she would know that. It was part of what was between them.

He tossed the attendant a bill and slid beneath the wheel again. It was a short run to the exit nearest Lois' address, and he rolled down the ramp smoothly, made the few blocks to West End in minutes, swung left, and hit three green lights before pulling in to the curb just beyond the modern brick apartment building.

There was a quiet and pleasant lobby that had about it a discreet look of minding its own business and allowing the tenants to mind theirs without interference from the management. The desk and switchboard, for instance, were off in one corner and sheltered by potted plants so visitors could enter and go directly to the self-service elevator without announcing themselves or being seen by curious eyes if they wished.

Wayne nodded with gratification when he noted the layout. It was so exactly what a successful career woman, "moderately chaste but not a prude," would select for herself. Tonight, Wayne turned aside to ask the switchboard operator the number of Miss Elling's apartment, but it was pleasant to know there would be no one to check on the time of his departure, and that in the future he would be able to come and go unnoticed.

Indeed, the girl on the switchboard displayed the acme of well-bred disinterest in Miss Elling's male visitor. She sat with her back to the small desk where Wayne paused, and did not turn her head when he said, "Miss Lois Elling, please?"

"Do you wish me to ring her, or would you prefer to go right up?" Her voice was pleasant and friendly, though impersonal.

"I'd like to go up, please."

"Number Six B. At the end of the corridor on your right as you leave the elevator."

Wayne thanked her and went to the elevator. It was large and modern, and ascended smoothly when he pressed the button marked 6.

At the end of the corridor to the right, there was a large silver B on the closed wooden door. Wayne put his finger on the bell and pressed it lightly. He heard a faint ringing inside, and waited with fast-beating heart for the door to open. Would she be already dressed in the black negligee that a man named Bill Johnson had given her for Christmas five years ago and which she had never yet worn? Or would she be saving that for . . . ?

When there was no answer to his ring after a full minute, Wayne smiled wryly and put his finger on the bell again and held it for a long time. Perhaps he had interrupted her in the middle of one of her nightly hot baths.

He hoped so. What was it she had said in her "letter" about jumping out of the tub and running in and dripping water on the white rug?

That would be a nice way to discover her this first night. Damned nice. It would do away with any formalities. The slender body dewy-fresh, pink and glowing from the hot water . . .

The smile faded into a frown as another minute went by without response. He didn't really mean the frown. Lois was exacting a small compensation, he surmised, for her rashness in throwing herself at him with that typewritten declaration in the office. She had blushed and burned when he read the words. Now she was making him burn a little, taking her own sweet time about coming to the door. After all, it must seem to her that he hadn't been overly impetuous about keeping the date.

Unthinkingly, as almost anyone will, he dropped his hand to the doorknob and turned it. He was surprised when the door swung open to his touch. Then the surprise faded and was replaced by amusement. That was like her, he thought. To leave the way open for him to come to her. To tantalize him a trifle and even, perhaps, to allow him to walk away disappointed if he didn't have the initiative to try the door and discover it unlocked.

Wayne closed the door quietly behind him and looked about the clean, bright, low-ceilinged living room with eager interest. Nothing particularly remarkable about the furnishing or décor—unlike the Gingham Girl's place in that respect, and infinitely more appealing and charming because of its unassuming simplicity. A wholly feminine room that somehow managed to reflect Lois' own honest eagerness for life. There were frilly butter-yellow curtains at the windows that gave just the needed touch of brightness to the moss-rose petit point of an heirloom sofa, and—Wayne smiled appreciatively as he recognized it—a shaggy white rug in front of a small table holding her telephone.

There were three closed doors leading off the room, and there was silence. Morgan Wayne called, "Lois," not too loudly, and she did not reply.

He crossed the room in four strides and opened the door to her bathroom. His throat tightened queerly when he discovered it still steamy and fragrant from her recent use. A pale green floor mat lay damp and wrinkled beside the tub. A woolly bath towel hung limply damp over the edge of the tub. A huge round box of expensive dusting powder stood open, the big dusting puff inside.

Wayne stepped back and set his teeth together tightly as he observed faint powdery touches left by Lois' bare feet on the polished floor from the bathroom and leading to the closed door a few feet to the right.

He followed them to the door, thinking to himself happily, Like an eagle scout winning a merit badge, by God. Old Tracker Wayne on the scent. You can't elude me, woman!

He opened the door blithely.

Lois Elling lay on the bed. The spread had been turned back to a white linen sheet, and the filmy negligee was starkly black against the whiteness. She had taken it from its tissue wrappings as she had promised. She had bathed and powdered and dabbed herself with just a touch of perfume, and arrayed herself in the never-before-worn negligee and carefully arranged her supple body on the white sheet to wait for Morgan Wayne to come to her.

But she no longer waited for him.

Her face was framed in the soft fluffy nest of her chestnut hair. Her mouth was a red, grinning slash from ear to ear.

Chapter Ten

THERE are shocks so sudden and deep that the human mind is unable to encompass them in the first instant of revelation. As in certain instances of intense physical pain, there is a merciful self-anesthesia that operates on the mind as well as on the body to carry one along for a few moments of adjustment before one accepts what is seen or felt.

The sight of Lois Elling slain on her bed had this effect on Morgan Wayne. His reactions were stunned into complete numbness. He saw her lying there, yet did not accept what he saw. His subconscious mind knew it was so, but his conscious mind rejected the knowledge.

It was some sort of grotesque masquerade. In a moment Lois would smile at him and sit up and beckon to him. There was blackness in front of his eyes and retching nausea in his belly as he stood rooted to the threshold in the cold rigidity of shock that would not allow his muscles to move. His teeth were set together so hard that his jaws began to ache, and when he shuddered into complete consciousness and forced his eyes to look at Lois again he discovered that his nails had gouged into his palms.

He moved then. He placed one foot before the other and crossed the short distance to the bed. He was cold now, as inhumanly aware and calculating as a machine, his frozen blue eyes probing down at the silent flesh that had so lately been pulsing with warmth and desire—for him.

It had been done recently. Very recently. Not more than ten or fifteen minutes had elapsed since death, Wayne's trained mind told him. Blood still oozed from the twin cruel gashes that extended from the sides of her mouth outward and downward. It was the most senseless and brutal job of mutilation Wayne had ever witnessed. No human hand could have held the knife that inflicted those slashes. It was the work of a monster. One who had enjoyed his work, had reveled in the sureness and nicety of his touch.

It would have been a horribly slow and painful death because the jugular vein had been carefully left untouched. Yet she lay so quietly and serene upon the white sheet. There was no contortion of limbs or features.

Wayne dropped to his knees and his fingertips gently explored the scalp beneath the mass of fluffy brown hair arranged so carefully about her face. He nodded grimly when he found a large swelling near the left ear. This explained the method of killing. He could see it all so clearly now, and a great racking sob came up into his throat as he visualized the scene.

Lois had taken her bath as usual, and tonight had carefully arrayed herself in the black negligee to wait for his coming. There had been the unexpected ring of her bell, her eager hurry to open the door and admit Morgan Wayne. But another man had confronted her there. A murderer with a sap ready and one sharp blow to be struck. Not a killing blow. No. The man who had done this was not disposed to kill mercifully or swiftly. A blow strong enough to halt any outcry and to render her unconscious so she could safely be carried into the bedroom and arranged in this dreadful mockery of anticipation for the careful wielding of a knife that she would not feel.

At least there had been that. She had died without knowing the mutilation inflicted.

Morgan Wayne's features tightened again and his eyes closed to slits when he noted a round spot of pink scalp showing through the fluffy hair near the back of her head. He bent closer to examine the spot and his senses reeled again at this further evidence of insensate brutality. A tuft of her silky brown hair had been torn out by the roots. There could be no doubt of it.

And Wayne saw why almost immediately.

Under the filmy blackness of the negligee covering her breasts there was discernible a dark stain of crimson. Wayne ripped the garment apart and stared down unbelievingly at the small wad of brown hair soaked with Lois' own blood and placed carefully in the deep valley between the creamy breasts that were now growing cold.

It had been used as a crude paintbrush to daub two words across her smooth abdomen:

"LAY OFF."

Morgan Wayne rocked back on his heels and an animal grunt of sheer rage welled up from inside him.

He knew now.

Of course, he had known from the beginning. From the first awful moment when he saw her lying there. This could be the work of only one man. A man whom Priscilla Endicott had said wasn't human. A man who loved death for the sake of killing. Ugly and lingering death.

Yes, he had known from the first moment that he was witnessing the work of Hake Derr. But it was good to have the assumption verified. It was good to know that her death could be avenged immediately and without seeking further proof.

The letters crudely smeared in blood on her white flesh were all the proof Morgan Wayne needed. The two final F's were the pay-off. For the same hand had formed those letters that had scrawled the single obscene word in the spilled powder atop the Gingham Girl's dressing table.

Wayne, alone, knew that. No other person could possibly know. It was clever, too, Wayne acknowledged to himself. Damnably clever of Derr. To Morgan Wayne it was clearly a message, meant only for him and for him only to understand. To the police, when they found her body, it would indicate that this was an ordinary sexual murder. The work of a jealous lover triumphantly adjuring a rival to desist from his attentions.

Wayne got to his feet slowly. His face was relaxed now, his blue eyes wide and calm. He leaned down and drew up the top sheet to cover Lois' body, to hide the mutilated face, leaving only the closed eyes, smooth forehead framed by fluffy brown hair. For a timeless moment he looked down at her while grief and rage swelled like an intolerable expanding ball within his chest. With only her eyes showing above the sheet, softly closed this way with long lashes brushing the smooth cheek, she looked as she might have looked with her head pillowed in the crook of his arm in sweet exhaustion.

He bent and touched his lips to her forehead, cooling now and glowing with the indefinable pallor of death. And as he did so he swore an oath that was not formed in words, but etched in acid on his soul. An oath that her killer would die by his hands, and soon. Derr's identity was his secret. It would remain his secret. Let the police discover her body in the natural course of events. Long before they could possibly get on the right trail, Morgan Wayne swore to himself she would be avenged.

Nothing else mattered now. Letty Hendrixon and the problem of Durtol Drugs were swept out of his mind by the consuming determination that now gripped him.

He turned and groped his way out of the death room, found the tiny kitchenette, and felt a new lump forming in his throat when he looked down somberly at a tray on the small table containing a bottle of bonded bourbon, a siphon bottle, two empty highball glasses standing side by side and a bowl of half-melted ice cubes.

Lois' preparations for the evening they were to have spent together. Further mute evidence of the manner in which she had planned to welcome him. He reached woodenly for the bottle and his corded fingers tightened on the neck of it. Then they relaxed and he took his hand away.

No. He wanted to be stone-cold sober for the job ahead of him. Nothing to dull a single sensory fiber of his body.

For the first time in his life Morgan Wayne wanted to kill—ached for the pleasure of taking life from another human being. And as he turned away from the kitchen, leaving the tray sitting there untouched, his mind began to work again with clarity for the first time since discovering Lois' body.

He knew it was the work of Hake Derr, and he knew it had been done simply as a warning to him. To lay off. To keep hands off the Durtol job. To stay away from the Hendrixons in the future.

Wayne stopped abruptly in the middle of the living room and narrowed his eyes to slits.

How had Hake Derr known about Lois Elling? How had he known Wayne would be here tonight to find the warning words smeared on her cold flesh in blood?

Priscilla Endicott? He had told her he had a date with his secretary. Just a careless phrase tossed over his shoulder while he hurried away to find Letty.

Had she repeated the words to Derr? Suppose she had? How had Derr known the identity of his secretary and where to find her? Lois had worked for him less than a week. Was it possible that Derr knew more about Wayne and his affairs than Wayne knew about him?

It was possible, of course. Wayne hadn't been discreet about making inquiries this past month. He hadn't meant to be discreet. From the beginning, he had known it would come to a showdown soon, and hadn't minded forcing the issue. He had known that Derr and his gang would get wind of his activities. And they had, of course. Priscilla had recognized his name instantly this afternoon. Her question "*What* are you?" proved that she was well aware of his interest in her lover.

So maybe they had been spying on him all this time while he was planted in the office spying on them and on the docked yacht that he had expected to be used as a prison for Letty.

That might explain how Derr had come to Lois Elling's

apartment so unerringly. And it would mean, of course, that Priscilla was as vicious as the others. That she had passed the information along to Derr to strike back at Wayne.

But there was one other possible explanation that could leave Priscilla out of it. And, surprisingly, Wayne found that he wanted desperately to leave her out. There was something about her that tore at his heartstrings when he contemplated her possible connivance in Lois' murder. Something about that first impression he got so strongly when he crossed to her at the piano and before they had spoken a word together. The vagrant and nebulous thought of home and mother that went along with her unabashed animality. That was an integral part of her appeal to a man's every sense. The brief picture that had flashed through his mind of climbing rosebushes and a white cottage with lighted windows.

Yes, he admitted frankly to himself that he *wanted* to leave Priscilla out of this nastiness. So he concentrated on the second possible explanation.

There had been others who knew he planned to see Lois Elling at her apartment this evening. Her phone call to Julius Hendrixon had stated that Wayne could be reached at her place later in the evening. How many people knew of that call? Julius, of course, and probably his wife. Probably John Durtol III also. And possibly the family attorney.

From the first, Wayne had felt positive there was someone behind Hake Derr in his bold attempt to seize control of Durtol Drugs by kidnaping Letty to force the sale of a block of stock to him. Could it be one of those four?

Wayne shook his head slowly as conjecture after conjecture raced through his mind. Julius, who had married into the firm and didn't own any stock but who was in active control of the management? It was a distinct possibility. He, above all others, would be in a position safely to manipulate the corporation's affairs to realize huge profits from diverting certain drugs into illegitimate channels. But that would mean profits to the stockholders. To his brother-in-law and his wife. And could a man conceivably help to plan the kidnaping of his own daughter in order to force his wife and brother-in-law to give up their blocks of stock?

It was possible, Wayne conceded grimly to himself. Particularly if such a move could force the sale of John's stock to some dummy owned by Hendrixon. He could be foolish enough to believe it was safe. To have extracted a promise from her kidnapers that the girl would be treated well and returned unharmed . . . Not exactly a fatherly thing to do, but when a man let himself get dragged into a thing like this he left his conscience behind him.

The mother was a less likely prospect, Wayne thought, but then he recalled the odd look on Mrs. Hendrixon's face and in her eyes on a couple of occasions and he didn't know. Of course, she owned the stock and could, presumably, dispose of it as she wished, so that seemed to take away the motivation from her, but it was possible there were some legal strings attached to it of which Wayne was unaware.

That was something that would have to be looked into.

Attorney Carson would know about that. But he was also suspect. Of all four, he was in the best position to have planned such a coup and to profit most from it. John Durtol III was the least likely, Wayne decided swiftly, remembering the weak chin and languid manner of the young man. Again, he had his own block of stock, which he could, presumably, turn over to racketeers if he wished to give them control. And kidnaping his own niece seemed an absurd device to accomplish what he could do so much more easily in a legitimate way.

Yet they were the four persons outside of the Gingham Girl who could conceivably have known that Morgan Wayne would be in this apartment tonight. If one of them were the mastermind behind the plan, it wouldn't have been difficult for him to pass on the information to Hake Derr for him to use as he had.

All of these thoughts and questions raced through Wayne's mind in a matter of seconds while he paused irresolute in Lois Elling's living room.

He put them from his mind almost as swiftly as they entered it. There was something more important to be attended to right now.

Wayne strode to the two doors leading into bathroom and bedroom and carefully wiped his prints from the doorknobs. He hesitated a moment, trying to think of anything else he might have touched, and recalled the whisky bottle. Another moment took care of that, and this time he didn't pause in the living room on his way out.

He rubbed both knobs of the outer door and closed it gently behind him, and gave the push button a hasty swipe as he went past toward the elevator.

The Gingham Gardens was his first objective. He seriously doubted that he would find Hake Derr there, but it was his only point of contact. Priscilla might know, as she had known his whereabouts that afternoon. And this time Morgan Wayne knew he would force the information out of her smooth throat with his two hands if necessary.

But he hoped it wouldn't be necessary.

Chapter Eleven

As he left the apartment house on West End Avenue, Wayne had more reason than before to be pleased by the privacy of the lobby and the lack of curiosity of the switchboard operator. Since she hadn't turned her head to look at him when he asked the number of Lois' apartment, it would be impossible for her to give any sort of description of him to the police. And right now Wayne didn't want any police interference with his movements.

Also, he was inwardly pleased with the thought that it was quite unlikely that Hake Derr could be identified either. Morgan Wayne was the only one who knew, and he wanted that secret to remain his own for a little time, at least. He didn't need much time. Just long enough to come face to face with Hake Derr.

He got in the borrowed Hudson and drove southward, rigid behind the wheel, but in no hurry now. His first surge of blind, killing rage had spent itself. The hot lust for vengeance had changed to a cold and more deadly emotion because it was reasoned and relentless. He would take chances, yes, but they would be coldly calculated chances. Both mind and body were tuned to the highest pitch of precision as he neared the Gingham Gardens. He could afford no mistakes this night. Not for his own sake, but for Lois Elling's.

He drove carefully and at a moderate speed to Fifty-second Street, turned eastward, and began watching ahead for a parking lot close to his objective. He found one on the left side of the street less than a block from the Gingham Gardens and pulled into the driveway, which was not quite blocked with cars.

An attendant sauntered forward as he got out, and

Wayne handed him the keys with a ten-dollar bill. He said curtly, "I may be ten minutes or three hours. And I may be in one hell of a hurry to get going when I do come back. The ten is for keeping this hack in a space open to the street and headed out."

The attendant said, "You bet, mister. Any time till two A.M."

Wayne nodded and walked away in long strides toward the life-sized oil painting on the sidewalk, with a red spotlight on it now to attract passers-by.

He slowed as he approached the cellar joint, noting that it occupied the entire subbasement of a one-story brownstone separated from its neighbors by a lane not more than two feet wide. Next door as he approached was a closed florist shop with a lighted window display, and Wayne paused in front of it, pretending an interest in the floral arrangements while he studied the first-floor layout of the next building. He carefully recalled climbing the stairs to Priscilla's apartment, and realized that her bedroom would be the front corner room on this side.

There was light behind the curtained windows. He realized that didn't necessarily mean it was occupied at the moment, but it was a hopeful sign. He chose a moment when the doorman was helping a drunken couple into a cab and the sidewalk was deserted, slid forward casually between the buildings, and made his way to the back. Here was an alley entrance to the kitchen, as he had been certain there would be, the door standing invitingly ajar and with the brightly lighted kitchen on the left. Wayne paused outside the door and watched a white-capped chef stirring a huge pot of soup on the range while two busboys come staggering in under heavy-laden trays that they clatteringly unloaded at the sink beyond his line of vision.

Choosing a moment when no one faced in his direction, Wayne entered and went unhurriedly past the open kitchen door, following a dimly lit hall to a closed wooden door at the end. It was locked, but he took the knob firmly and braced himself, put steady and increasing pressure with his shoulder against the door, and the flimsy catch gave way. His tight hold of the knob prevented him from catapulting forward, and he found himself in the narrow corridor with the flight of stairs leading upward that he had climbed with Priscilla that afternoon.

Hot piano music and the laughter and din of a night spot doing good business came at him with a rush from the other end of the corridor as Wayne closed the door behind him. At the far end toward the front he saw the figure of Willie Sutra with his back toward Wayne.

He had the look of being posted there as a guard to prevent entrance to the stairway, and this gave Wayne further hope that Priscilla might be upstairs. With someone, perhaps. Even with Hake Derr, possibly, though he refused to hope for that much luck.

His right hand was in the side pocket of his linen jacket fondling the butt of a large-caliber gun as he climbed the stairs cautiously so as to make no sound that would attract Sutra's attention.

The same stairs he had climbed this afternoon so close behind Priscilla's willowy body. Just this afternoon, that had been. Only a few hours past. But this time there was no enticing rustle of a taffeta skirt. There was no woman smell to come back to his nostrils warmly, no promise of delight when the upward climb was ended. Tonight there was silence and the subtle aura of death on the stairway.

At the top of the stairs, Wayne stopped in front of the door Priscilla had unlocked that afternoon and lifted the gun from his right-hand pocket. He turned the knob and entered the unlocked living room with the chartreuse draperies at the far end.

The long room was empty. The door into the bedroom stood open as it had that afternoon, and Priscilla Endicott stood on one foot in front of the vanity mirror, leaning forward with the other foot resting on the low stool while she carefully drew a stocking upward over the shapely ankle and calf. The other leg was already stockinged and she wore a narrow garter belt. Nothing else. Her back was toward Wayne.

She straightened slowly as the stocking came up, and Morgan Wayne closed the door behind him after thumbing the catch to set the night lock.

The tiny click it made as the door closed brought Priscilla's head around over her shoulder while she was still in a half crouch. She was as impossibly lovely as ever. White-faced now and staring, her eyes round and enormous with surprise and fright, caught in that posture for an instant like a startled fawn face to face suddenly with a crouching panther.

Wayne dropped the heavy gun into his pocket and strolled forward without speaking. His first movement released Priscilla's spellbound muscles. Her head jerked back and she straightened swiftly and snatched up a green silk robe from the dressing table and flung it about her shoulders. Entering the bedroom, Morgan Wayne told her evenly, "You don't need to cover it up, Priscilla. I've come for something else entirely this time."

Priscilla Endicott turned slowly to face him, drawing the edges of the thin robe tight together in front. Her face was still white and she spoke as evenly as he, but flames danced in the translucent green eyes and her tone was so low as to be almost guttural:

"What do you mean by something *else* this time? What did you want from me this afternoon except what you got?"

He sat down on the edge of the still unmade bed and regarded her levelly. "You know what I wanted this afternoon. I still want it. But not right now."

"And not this afternoon either." Her voice rose and

she almost choked with rage. "Did your goddamned secretary appreciate what you walked out of here with?"

Morgan Wayne said, "This is wasting time. You know how fast Hake Derr got here after you phoned him. There wouldn't have been time."

"But you didn't know that," she raged at him. "I don't know how the hell he heard me say that to you over the phone, but—"

"*I* know," Wayne interrupted her. "And I think you do too. I think you tried to set me up for him, and when that failed you handed him my secretary instead." He got to his feet as he spoke and moved toward her, his face rocklike, blue eyes hooded and coldly watchful.

She shrank away from him instinctively. "Your secretary?" she gasped. "I didn't . . ."

"I think you did, Priscilla." Wayne put both hands on her shoulders and his face was inches from hers. "I'm not sure of it yet. If I were I'd break your neck. When I do find out, I *will* break your neck. But before I do that I'm going to take that lovely, wanton body of yours as it's never been taken before."

His fingers tightened roughly on her shoulders. His voice was low and hoarse, charged with the two most elemental passions of man—desire and anger.

Priscilla Endicott did not flinch from the hurting pressure of his fingers. Her eyes were wide now, and shining. Her lips parted as the breath came in and out more swiftly. "Promise me you'll do that, Morgan Wayne. Then you can break my neck if you still want to."

Her mouth was there, waiting for him. Her body was taut and quivering, waiting for him.

Wayne set his teeth and let go of her shoulders with a little shove that sent her back against the low dressing table. He turned and took three steps across the room and wheeled to face her at this safer distance. He asked quietly, "How long did Derr stay this afternoon?"

"Only a few minutes." There was a singing sort of calmness in her voice. "He expected to find you in bed with me and went into a rage because I had let you get away. Are you really another gangster, Morgan, trying to move in on Hake's racket? Whoever you are and whatever you want, stay away from Hake, for God's sake. I'm telling you . . ."

"There's only one thing I want you to tell me, Priscilla. Where is Hake Derr?"

"I don't know," she replied promptly. Too promptly? Wayne wondered. "He went out of here swearing to carve you up in little pieces and I don't know where he is."

"But you can tell me where I might find him."

"No. He doesn't really trust me yet." Her voice was low and troubled. "I've never seen him any place except here. I don't know anything else about him."

"You know what his real business is." Wayne threw the words at her as though they were rocks.

She lifted her head defiantly and spat out, "Of course I know. Why in hell else do you think I'd let a lunk like that in my bed?"

"To get stuff from him?" Wayne's voice was disbelieving. "I don't believe it," he said flatly.

"No," she told him contemptuously. "Not to get stuff from him. My God, I can pick up anything I want in this town without sleeping with the head guy. Aside from that, I don't go for it personally."

"Then *why*, Priscilla?"

"Because Hake Derr's in the money. Real money." Her lips thinned against her teeth and she loosened the edges of the green robe to hold both hands out in front of her with the fingers tightly balled into fists. "That's what I'm out for," she told him fiercely. "Mazuma. Wads of it. And Hake's on his way up. He's got a deal on now that'll put him up along with the goddamned Rockefellers and Morgans. And that's where I want to be."

"You've got a pretty good little racket of your own right here," Wayne told her soberly.

"Chicken feed."

"Even a cellar joint like this is cleaner than peddling dope to school kids," Wayne said wearily.

"Hake don't peddle it. There's plenty of others to do that work, and if he didn't furnish them someone else would. What are you horning in on Hake for if dope money is too dirty for you to handle?"

Morgan Wayne hesitated a long moment before replying. He was vaguely conscious that Priscilla's robe had fallen open in front, but he was more concerned with studying her face and intonations and trying to figure the angles than in the white flesh she was showing him. A lot might depend on how he answered her. If it were true that she was only interested in money and not in Derr himself—and if he could convince her that with a little help from her he might soon be in a position to take over Derr's business with its huge profits—the chances were that she would be eager to play along.

But somehow, something rang false in her statements. There was that first intuitive feeling he had about her that afternoon. He couldn't drive himself to believe she was all bad. A wanton, yes. Tough-minded and with an eye to the main chance. She'd never have got where she was now without those attributes. But for her to have cold-bloodedly tied up with a drug racketeer like Hake Derr simply to feather her own nest and for no other personal reason was more than Wayne could accept. She was lying to him now, he thought grimly. Following orders from Hake Derr and trying to draw him out into the open.

He said finally, "Maybe I'm changing my mind about horning in on Derr. From what I hear around, this thing he's got on is big enough so he might be able to use a partner to handle some of the angles. Tell me where he is and I'll talk it over with him."

"I told you I didn't know." Suddenly Priscilla's voice was listless and disinterested. She glanced down at the spreading edges of her robe and drew them together mechanically. Not as though it mattered much, but as an indication that the interview was ended.

"So you've told me," Morgan Wayne agreed. "So you'll phone him as soon as I walk out of here. That's O.K. I want you to. Tell him I'll be around. Tonight."

He turned about and strode out of the bedroom. He didn't look back as he crossed the living room of Priscilla's apartment and there was only silence behind him.

He went out unhurriedly and down the stairs. He moved surely and silently on the balls of his feet toward the front exit, where Willie Sutra still stood facing away from him.

The noise of the piano and of loud laughter beyond Willie drowned the sound of his coming. He lifted a heavy gun from his pocket as he neared the man, and he paused behind him to swing the loaded cylinder and short barrel against the right side of Willie's head just above the ear.

Willie went to the floor without making a sound.

Wayne pocketed his gun and calmly stepped over the limp figure. If anyone in the long dim room noted the incident, there was something about Morgan Wayne as he crossed to the front, looking neither to the right nor to the left, something about the set of his wide shoulders, the implacable grimness of his face and the icy coldness of his eyes, that prevented any interference.

Wayne went out past the hat-check girl without seeing her and turned toward the parking lot where he had left the Hudson.

Chapter Twelve

MORGAN WAYNE drove north to 110th Street and parked at the curb. It was a cool night and he shivered a little in his linen suit as he got out of the Hudson. He turned the jacket collar up about his neck and let his heavy shoulders hunch forward in a sort of slouch, assuming a shambling and slightly furtive air as he walked half a block to "Flying Horse" Avenue. It was a mean little street with a few small shops lighted at this hour, and those who passed on the sidewalk moved purposefully and looked neither right nor left.

There was a dim street lamp halfway down the block, and Wayne stationed himself close to it so the bleared beams lighted his white suit plainly but kept his face shadowed.

He yawned openly at intervals, hunching his shoulders and shuddering as he did so, stretching out his arms and darting quick side glances in either direction.

Nothing happened for at least five minutes. Two men passed behind him on the sidewalk as though unconscious of his presence, and then a woman approached from his right. She slowed as she neared him, and Wayne went through his yawning routine again, noting with a side glance that she was drably dressed and staggering a trifle.

She stopped close behind him and asked in a furred voice that tried hard to sound coy and desirable, "Lookin' for somethin', mister?"

He turned slowly, rubbing the back of his hand across his mouth. "Not what you're peddling, sister."

She tossed her head archly and put one hand on her hip. "How d'yuh know if you don't take a try? Three ways for a fin ain't a bad deal, huh?"

"Beat it," snarled Wayne. "Ten ways for a buck wouldn't interest me right now."

"I getcha," she told him wisely. "Soon's you're fixed up you'll maybe want some. I'll be waitin' down to the gin mill yonder." She moved on, swaying her fat hips so flagrantly that she almost fell flat on her face.

Wayne faced around again and gave another yawn. He saw a thin, boyish figure step from a darkened doorway two hundred feet down the street and accost the prostitute. She spoke to him, then laughed and went on toward the lighted barroom a short distance beyond.

The other figure strolled toward Wayne. A thin-faced lad who didn't look older than fifteen, trying to put a swagger in his walk and with an unlighted cigarette drooping at a wise-guy angle from the corner of his mouth.

He passed Wayne without speaking, looking him over carefully and letting his footsteps get slower and slower as he went on, until he stopped thirty feet away, turned, and sauntered back while his hands went searchingly into his pockets. He stopped and asked past the cigarette, "Got a match, mister?"

Wayne nodded. He got a lighter from his pocket and held it so the boy could not fail to note the gold case, thumbed it to a flame, and held it out with shaking hands.

The lad bent to suck flame into his cigarette, twisting his head to look up at Wayne with narrowed, ferrety eyes. "You got the shakes, mister. What the hell? It ain't that cold."

"The monkey's on my back, kid," Wayne said huskily. "He's scratchin' like hell, but a punk like you wouldn't know about that."

"Think so, huh?" The boy grinned slyly and sucked smoke deep into his lungs. "I figured you was a customer when I seen yuh standin' here yawnin'. An' I knowed it fer sure when you give Three-Way Annie the turn-down." He became abruptly businesslike. "Which yuh want, mister? I got horse an' weed."

"Horse. How much you got?" Wayne put whining eagerness in his voice.

"I got five decks on me."

"That's O.K. for a starter, but look. I gotta have more. Lots more. I'm in a spot, see? Lammin' out of town where I maybe can't get it easy, and my own peddler, damn his lousy soul, is shacked up somewheres I can't reach him. I need twenty decks fast."

"Twenty decks of H? Jeez, mister, I ain't never pushed a wad like that before. A deck here an' a deck there . . . you know how it is. Just enough to pay for my own shots."

"But you can get it," Wayne pressed eagerly. He rubbed knuckles into both eyes and sniffled loudly. "I'll pay extra because I got to have it fast."

"Sure, I can get it O.K. But how do I know . . ."

"Here." Wayne fumbled in his pocket with trembling fingers and drew out a crumpled fifty-dollar bill. "Gimme your five decks now and keep that bill for an advance against the other fifteen. How soon can you get it?"

The boy looked at the bill and whistled with surprise. He dug into his pocket and pulled out five small paper packets and handed them over with a sly grin. "I guess you ain't no narcotics guy, all right. No cop'd jar loose with half a C when he could do it for ten. Take me about forty minutes, mister. Where'll you be?"

Morgan Wayne slid four of the packets in his pocket and was fumbling eagerly with the fifth as though in a hurry to get some good from it. He nodded down the street and said, "How about meeting me in that bar?"

"Sure." The boy's wizened grin became a leer. "Where Annie hangs out, huh? After a shot she'll mebby look better to you. See you there in forty minutes."

Chapter Thirteen

Case history of Johnny Harlon, aged fifteen, 1348——Street, New York City, as wire-recorded by Sergeant Nickerson of the New York City Police Department's Narcotic Squad.

"You start with reefers, see? They're a sort of cigarette, only different. You smoke them different. You suck the smoke in with lots of air, all the way in till your guts are floating—and pretty soon you're floating too. You're high, mister, and you never had it so nice. Everybody's your pal and the girls all love you. Anything you want is yours for the asking—or taking. You can do anything, see? Rip an automobile tire in two with your bare hands if you want to, beat hell out of a cop twice as big. That's how it seems. You ain't afraid of nothing and there ain't nothing to be afraid of. Things taste better'n they ever did before, and smell better. And if you're with a girl, it lasts a million years and it's so good you can't stand it. You die on her and then come back to life and you ain't dead at all but alive like you never was alive before. That's the way reefers do you at first.

"But next morning you're crawling in hell, mister. You're down at the bottom and there ain't no way out. You itch all over and your nose and eyes burn and run water, and your throat's dry and rasping like a charred crust of bread. You lay there wherever you are and vomit all over yourself and it's like you're a pig in a pen, but it don't matter none. Nothing matters except getting some more and getting back alive again.

"So that goes on and you need more'n more for your lift, and pretty soon there just ain't enough kick to it and you got to have something stronger, and then you start sniffing the powder and that's O.K. for a while, but then it gets just the same as the other and pretty soon you end up like anybody else and start main-lining. That's punching a hole in the vein and taking the heroin hot into the blood straight from a medicine dropper. You get the jolt, mister, before you can count five, and it's real good. Better'n ever before, because now you're fixed so you can't do without it, and that's O.K. as long as it lasts, but it keeps lasting shorter and shorter and you got to get a fix oftener and oftener till pretty soon you got to have it three-four times a day and it takes fifteen or twenty bucks a day to keep you right.

"Where'm I gonna get that kind of money? Not by working. I can't get no job to pay me like that, and besides, I got to stay in school, and even if I run away I ain't in no good shape to hold down a job.

"So all I can do is start stealing because I got to have the dough. Or maybe hang around the queer joints and be some brownie's boy.

"Sure, I tried 'em both, but neither one worked good. I started grabbing stuff from stores, but the bastards you got to sell to only give you maybe a tenth of what it's worth and you never do have enough jack, and then I tried the other, but the queers you run into mostly expect you to give it to 'em instead of selling it.

"Then the pusher where I get my horse says why don't I turn peddler myself, and he sets me up in business for free. I know all the kids in school, see? So he gives me reefers to pass out free and get them started just like I did. And I don't mind none by this time because I think why shouldn't them other punks be like I am, so I hand the reefers around, and then pretty soon start showing 'em how to main-line with heroin for a real kick. That's free, too, at first, but not very long, you bet. Soon's them others get to where they got to have it, I'm the only one around where they know to get it. So I'm right in there peddling it to them and it's easy money and it's their tough luck where they get the jack to pay me.

"So I did real good at first. I was what they call a mule. That's a delivery boy for this pusher, and he pays me just enough for my own shots, but that's all right because I don't need nothing else.

"But I go on the nod so steady I get so I can't remember nothing, and I'm going nuts from wanting it between jolts and stealing it from my own customers, and even that ain't enough, so finally I get arrested when I kill that old man in the candy store.

"You said I killed him, anyhow. I don't know for sure. I didn't go to kill him. I just wanted money for a deck of H. Honest to God, I don't remember hitting him with the rock you say I had in my hand. I just needed the H real bad, that's all, and I had to get it some way."

The boy who contracted to "take the monkey off" Morgan Wayne's back could have been Johnny Harlon a short time before Johnny made his kill. Any one of New York City's six thousand adolescent dope addicts could have been Johnny Harlon; that is, their personal case histories parallel Johnny's step by step except that the girls usually wind up selling themselves on the streets to get money for their daily dope rations, and except that most are discovered and arrested before taking the final step of committing murder to obtain the money they cannot do without.

Fifteen minutes after the boy had left Morgan Wayne under the street lamp, he turned up in a dirty gin mill in the San Juan Hill district only a block off the Hudson River. He stood just inside the door nervously looking around the smoke-filled room until he got the nod from a thin, greasy-faced man sitting alone at a table in the back.

For props, Poppy McMooney had a beer glass and a racing form in front of him. The form sheet was a week old. The glass had suds caked inside in dry rings. Poppy was a pusher who attended strictly to business.

The boy slid into the seat across from him and leaned forward intently, talking in a low voice. "Twenty decks, Poppy," he ended excitedly. "Twenty decks all at onct, he wants."

"Yeah? How you know he's on the level?"

"Hell, he *needs* it, Poppy. You shoulda seen 'im."

"A guy like that," said Poppy distrustfully, "with money to pay for twenty decks, he don't have to stand out under no street light hopin' some mule will come along to fix him up. If he's on the stuff, he's got his own supply where he gets it steady."

"Sure, but like I told you, he's takin' it on the lam outta town an' his regular peddler ain't around. I swear he's O.K., Poppy."

"You'd say that about anybody, Alvin. You're so red-eyed crazy for H you'd sell twenty decks to the Mayor. I been thinkin' about dropping you, Alvin. You're gettin' so damned jittery . . ."

"You wouldn't do that, Poppy! I got to have it. You know I got to have it."

"I know," grumbled Poppy McMooney. "That's why I don't trust you. How you know he didn't say twenty decks so you'd get excited and make a home run for me, with him follerin' on your heels?"

"Aw, no, Poppy. It ain't nothin' like that. I cased him good before I fused him. Hell, he had the shakes so bad he even turned down a dame. You know how it is when a guy needs some horse."

"Where'd you say this customer is?" grunted Poppy. "I'll take a look at him."

"You can do that right now." Morgan Wayne's incisive voice cut into the conversation. He stood beside the back table with the bulk of his body cutting off the pusher and his adolescent "mule" from the view of the others in the barroom.

Poppy McMooney jerked back and swiveled his long neck to look up at the stranger, and the boy shrank away in fright, his jaw sagging open as he stuttered, "You—you follered me?"

Wayne nodded without looking at him. In a not unkindly voice, he advised, "Blow, son. Get out of here fast and don't come back." Wayne took a side step to let the frightened youth slither past and out of the room, then he smiled slightly and explained to Poppy, "No use letting a punk like that in on a real business deal." He brought a hand carelessly from his pocket showing a wad of bills. "I can use plenty where I'm going. I said twenty decks to the kid because I knew any more would scare the pants off him. How much you got stashed that I can get in a hurry?"

Poppy stared at the wadded bills and saw they were a mixture of twenties and fifties and hundreds. He gulped and his eyes glistened and avarice overcame his caution. There was class written all over this customer. Not at all the sort of addict Poppy generally dealt with. If he was really desperate for a lot of stuff to move out of town fast, the chances were he wouldn't haggle about price. "I got a good supply," he mumbled. "Don't know exactly how much, but . . ."

"Let's get it and see. Goddamn it, man!" exploded Wayne. "I'm in a hurry. I got to be through the Tunnel and into Jersey in half an hour. That's why I had to work it this way. Where you got it?"

The sight of so much money mesmerized Poppy McMooney. He pushed himself erect and said thickly, "Right upstairs. I got me a room here."

Wayne nodded with satisfaction and said, "Fine." He followed Poppy out the rear and up a flight of stairs to the two small rooms above. Poppy carefully unlocked an expensive Yale lock and opened one of the doors. He flipped on a ceiling light and Wayne gave him a shove that sent him staggering to his knees on the floor.

He jerked out a startled "What the hell?" scrambling to his feet and whirling to see Wayne pulling the door shut and turning to face him.

All trace of amiability had departed from Wayne's face now that he was alone in a closed room with the peddler. His left hand was bunched in his coat pocket and his voice was glacial. "I just want one thing from you, and it isn't dope."

"Yeah?" snarled Poppy.

Wayne said, "Yeah. I'm not a dick. I don't give one goddamn about you and your stinking racket of peddling to school kids. I'm on my way to see Hake Derr, and you're the next step up."

"Hake Derr?" wheezed Poppy.

"Don't tell me you never heard of him."

"Sure, I heard of Hake." Poppy was rapidly regaining his self-assurance. "But he's one of the top men. I never had no dealings with him."

"Where do you get your stuff?"

Poppy made a vague gesture. "I took all the stock off a guy. Don't even know his name. He's outta business now."

Morgan Wayne stepped in swiftly with a backhanded blow across the mouth that sent the peddler to the floor again. He lifted himself on one elbow, spitting teeth and snarling venomously, "That's new bridgework, goddamn it. I paid—"

"I'm just getting started," Wayne interrupted placidly. He kicked at Poppy McMooney, bent forward swiftly as the peddler went down again, caught one thin wrist and twisted it behind his back, and lifted him up by that leverage while a screech of anguish started from Poppy's mouth.

Wayne's other hand slapped the sound back down his throat before it really got started. He shook his head and explained matter-of-factly, "I don't mind killing you except that it would delay matters for me. Who's the highest man in the racket you can reach this time of night?"

"I tell you I don't know—" Blood was streaming from Poppy's broken nose and a two-inch slit in his cheek. He gagged over the words as Wayne's fingers closed relentlessly about his scrawny neck to hold him upright while he put a steady upward pressure on the arm twisted behind Poppy's back.

"I can't tell what I don't know. My God, you'll break my arm. For gossake . . ."

Morgan Wayne laughed thinly in his face. "Of course I'll break your arm. And then the other one. After that, I'll twist them both off and beat you to death with them. Don't you think I'd enjoy that?"

The absolutely horrible thing to Poppy was the stranger's complete lack of emotion as he spoke and put increasing pressure on the tortured arm. His voice was controlled and pleasant and thoughtful, and carried the deadly ring of sincere conviction.

"I'd like to take every dope peddler in New York in my two hands and break him into little pieces," Wayne went on. "Every despicable hunk of scum in human form who deals in the degradation of children for profit. Unfortunately, that's a large chore for one man, but please don't get the idea I want you to talk fast. The longer you hold out, the better I like it."

He inexorably tightened the pressure on Poppy's windpipe as he spoke, cutting off any sound except a faint whimpering moan while the man's arm moved upward between his shoulder blades inch by inch and the pain caused his eyes to protrude while face and body writhed and contorted in Wayne's merciless grasp.

There was an abrupt, splintering crack as the elbow ligaments gave way. Wayne let go with both hands and stepped back dispassionately to consider the groaning figure that flopped on the floor in front of him.

"That's just one arm. I'm getting to Hake Derr tonight and you're pointing the finger that'll put me on my way. Perhaps I'd better start on the fingers of the other hand," he went on meditatively. "One by one they'll last longer." He stopped to grab the wrist of the unbroken arm, but Poppy jerked it away from him, moaning and slobbering:

"No, no. Don't hurt me no more. I'll tell yuh anything. Mother of God, don't touch me again."

"I doubt whether she'll pay much attention to you," Wayne said coldly. "Start talking and make it good."

Poppy McMooney was huddled on the floor with his face in his hands. He began sputtering out words intermingled with sobs and Wayne leaned close to hear more clearly. He heard "Vito" and "The Barber," and a light showed in the coldness of his blue eyes for the first time since he had opened the door to Lois Elling's bedroom. By sheer chance, he had struck it lucky when the boy led him to Poppy McMooney. Most of the pushers like Poppy dealt only with one small dealer who was, in turn, supplied by a little bigger dealer, who in turn . . .

But Poppy was evidently a pusher who was very much on the way up. Vito "The Barber" Saietta was a name that Morgan Wayne recognized. One of the half-dozen big-shot middlemen in the city who bought raw heroin direct from the syndicate, processed it, and passed it on to distributors. It was one chance in a thousand that a peddler of Poppy's type would have any contact with The Barber.

Wayne dragged the cringing man to his feet and flung him into a chair. He said, "Stop your goddamned sniveling and talk so I can understand you. Where do I find Vito?"

Tears and blood were coursing down Poppy's face. His left arm was grotesquely twisted and he leaned far forward to hold it pressed tightly against his body in the angle between torso and limbs. He avoided Wayne's gaze and moaned:

"No. I dunno nothin'. I said that to make you stop. I just heard him mentioned."

"Do we have to start this all over again?" Wayne asked wearily. "You'll give me The Barber, or you'll die right here. Slow . . . and messy."

"But they'll kill me. I swear I—"

"And I'll kill you if you don't. It's a tough spot to be in," Wayne agreed unemotionally. "Make up your mind fast, because I can't wait."

Poppy knew this strangely inhuman man meant it. In the depths of his soul, he knew this was no bluff. His broken arm told him that, if Wayne's eyes and his voice weren't convincing enough.

"Near Columbus Circle," he grated through tightly set teeth. "I dunno the exact address. There's a barbershop an' he lives upstairs. I wasn't there but once."

"You're going again tonight." Wayne caught him by his good arm and jerked him roughly erect.

"My God, no! I'll give you the address, but if they ever find out—"

"They'll bump you. I know. Come on with me." Wayne shoved him toward the door.

Chapter Fourteen

Vito Saietta was an old Unione Siciliano man. A dependable and unimaginative worker, he had progressed upward in the dreaded organization through the years and through many phases of lawlessness to his present enviable and comparatively safe position as an independent purchaser of raw heroin smuggled in from South America, which he cut with milk sugar and sold at wholesale to gross himself a comfortable $40,000 per kilo. Not having to cut Uncle Sam in on income taxes, Vito netted himself a very comfortable living even though a large percentage of his take did have to go out in bribes to various higher-ups in the police department and persons with political influence.

He was known throughout the trade as The Barber, and the nickname was accompanied by a sly grin when used by old-timers who knew the circumstances under which it had been bestowed.

Vito Saietta actually was a barber in the beginning, and he still maintained his dingy one-man shop in the basement of the building in which he lived near Columbus Circle. But Vito didn't work in the shop now except on very, very rare occasions. Long ago, before he had become a prosperous businessman respected by his associates and envied by those who accepted a share of his dirty profits to allow him to stay in business—before all that had come about, Vito had been an excellent craftsman and a very hard toiler at his chosen trade.

His small shop was admirably situated for the purpose it served. One went down a flight of concrete steps from the sidewalk to a wooden door with a faded and inconspicuous sign above: "Vito's Shop." One opened the door, if it were not locked, and entered a six-by-eight cubbyhole to be greeted pleasantly by the beaming and bright-eyed proprietor. If the customer simply requested a haircut or shave or both, his wants were attended to with neatness and dispatch and he was sent on his way with no reason to suspect the more important business that was sometimes transacted in the tiny shop.

But if the customer were a stranger and knocked twice on the door before entering, and then told Vito, "Enrico [or Pugs or Mickey—the names changed from year to year owing to the inevitable turnover in the Unione Siciliano hierarchy] sent me here to get a shave," then Vito would beam more happily and his small eyes would glisten with a certain liquid warmth, for he was proud of his art with the razor and of the special treatment he accorded these favored customers.

As the man settled himself in the chair, Vito unobtrusively slipped the heavy bolt on the inside of the wooden door to assure the needed privacy and carefully spread a heavy towel over the front of the customer while inquiring gravely about the health of his good friend Enrico (or Pugs or Mickey).

Then there was a special razor, carefully honed and stropped and kept in a velvet-lined case, which was lifted down with pride and placed ready at hand, the hot towel squeezed out and spread with care across the customer's face, and then the one swift movement of the razor across the exposed throat that was Vito's pride and his trade-mark.

There was never any fuss or bother about Vito's killings, and scarcely a single drop of blood escaped the two towels so strategically located to absorb the flow. There was a door at the back of the shop that led out into the furnace room, where the body could safely remain until evening, when a truck pulled up in the alley to receive it—and weeks later the body would turn up in a vacant lot somewhere in the Bronx or Queens.

That's how Vito had come to be known as The Bar-

ber, though few people today knew the real story behind the nickname. And it was on only very particular
occasions, now, that anyone was sent to Vito "for a
shave," because it had to be arranged beforehand so that
Vito would be in the shop and waiting for the victim.

But Vito didn't mind the scarcity of these occasions
now. He was an older man and content to turn the more
energetic aspects of the trade over to younger men. He
had his memories of past pleasures to live with him; he
had his thriving business, which he conducted zealously
and well from the first-floor apartment directly above
the barbershop; he had his pet goldfish and his comfortable, old-country wife, Rosa, who cooked his favorite
dishes for him and stayed unquestioningly in the kitchen
when he conducted his business in the front room.

Tonight Vito was at home, as usual. He anticipated a
quiet evening with no business interruptions and was
in his undershirt and slippers. The pleasantly pungent
odors of *orégano,* tomato sauce, and red peppers drifted
out through an open door from the kitchen. All was
peace in The Barber's well-ordered world. He puffed
composedly on a short, blackened pipe as he shuffled
about from one to another of the dozen round, old-
fashioned bowls of plump goldfish that stood on low
tables about the room. Each bowl had a miniature
Italian castle inside and the fish could swim lazily in and
out through the doors and windows. He was giving them
their supper of prepared fish food, and he stood content-
edly by each bowl after dropping a spoonful in, watching the fish dart about and suck the food in greedily as
it filtered down through the water to them.

There was a buzz from the outside bell. Vito lifted
shaggy black brows in surprise and took the stubby pipe
from his mouth. He was expecting no callers tonight.
If it was a business matter, there would be a short pause,
then two short buzzes, another pause, and then a single
long buzz.

His eyebrows lifted higher when two buzzes came after a brief pause. The only possibility was that one of the half-dozen large peddlers to whom Vito sold direct as a side line and for added profits had had a sudden large turnover and unexpectedly needed additional supplies. When the final long buzz sounded, Vito put down his box of fish food and wiped his hands on the front of his undershirt, moving on stumpy legs to the door to press the button releasing the outside catch. As he did so, the door to the kitchen was closed firmly from the other side. Vito nodded with satisfaction. Rosa had heard the signal, and like any obedient wife had closed the door so as not to disturb whatever business transactions were to be conducted. The door would remain closed until Vito himself opened it.

He heard the outer door open and footsteps coming down the hall to his door. He opened it and saw two men standing there. One was tall and thin and had a wool scarf around his neck and was holding it bunched up over his face so only his eyes showed over the scarf. The eyes were glazed with fright and with desperate and silent appeal as Vito met them. He vaguely recognized the man as a peddler with whom he had occasional dealings.

The other man was big and bareheaded. He wore a white suit and sport shoes, white shirt and black tie. All were of exceptional quality. Vito had been in the big money long enough to recognize quality, though he had never paid more than $39.95 for a suit in his life. The man's features were square and placid, as was the faint smile on his strong mouth. Only the eyes weren't placid. They were blue and hot. Somehow, you don't expect blue eyes to be hot. These eyes were hot with menace. And the heavy gun in the man's left hand was menacing, too.

Vito moved back a careful step or two without saying anything. The blood was pulsing through his temples, but he took a steady drag on his pipe and let none of his inner alarm show through. He was an old-timer who had survived more than his share of gang feuds and realignments by always being quick to sense the winning side and to shift to it faster than most. Right now, his one definite reaction was that the big man looked like a fellow Vito would like to have on his side.

The thin man turned to his companion and spoke in a curiously thick voice through the bunched-up scarf. "I done it, see? Can I beat it?"

The big man nodded and said casually, "Sure. Beat it." He did not take his eyes from Vito's face as the other hurried away. He followed Vito inside and glanced approvingly about the empty, shabby room. "Nobody else around?"

"Only my Rosa in the kitchen." Vito bobbed his bald head toward the closed door. He shuffled away and seated himself quietly in a rocking chair, folding stubby-fingered hands in his lap. Vito was good at waiting.

His caller dropped the gun into a side pocket. He said, "I'm Morgan Wayne."

Vito said, "So?" He looked down into the bowl of his pipe and poked a forefinger in to press the hot ashes down so it would draw better.

Wayne said, "I've got to see Hake Derr tonight."

Vito said nothing.

Wayne moved across the room to stand close to Vito. He thrust both hands into his trousers pockets and rocked back on his heels. His eyes were slitted but his face remained coolly impassive. "You're going to tell me where to find him, Vito."

Still Vito said nothing. He rocked placidly back and forth in the old-fashioned chair, his hands clasped in front of his round belly.

Wayne knew The Barber by reputation. He didn't believe the tactics he had used on Poppy would work on Vito. He glanced calculatingly about the room and noted the twelve round fishbowls with the beautifully wrought Italian castles inside and the plump goldfish swimming lazily about. He moved aside and looked down into one bowl with interest, saying over his shoulder, "Pretty things, aren't they?"

"You like fish?"

"Crazy about them. You too?"

"They are good friends," said Vito stolidly.

Wayne reached one big hand down into the water while Vito watched him with bulging eyes. There were three fish in the bowl. They weren't afraid of his hand in the water. They were accustomed, Wayne thought, to having Vito reach down and touch them.

He cupped one in his fingers without difficulty, pulled it dripping from the bowl, and turned about so Vito could see him.

He bit the head of the goldfish off with one crunch of strong teeth and began chewing on it.

Vito came out of his chair sputtering Italian expletives. Morgan Wayne held the quivering and headless body of the goldfish out to him and said thickly, "Have a bite yourself. I just like the heads."

The Barber made a lunge forward, as crazed with anger and horror as a father witnessing his child being torn limb from limb by wild animals.

Wayne laughed and flung the body of the goldfish in his face, tripping him as he did so, and jerking his own head aside to spit out the distasteful morsel from his mouth without Vito's seeing him.

Vito got to his knees with tears of supplication streaming down his fat face. "Please, you must not," he gasped. "So innocent, the fish! To eat them alive!"

"Very tasty," said Wayne, giving a final munch and pretending to gulp down a big swallow. "You must have three or four dozen of them in all these bowls. Fat and well fed, too." He cupped his hands together and turned to another of the bowls eagerly.

Vito scrambled to his feet and got in front of him. "For the love of our Saviour, no," he whimpered. "This Hake Derr. Why do you want to see him?"

"Maybe to make a deal." Wayne paused. "Maybe I'm taking over, Vito. I guess you've heard he loused up his big deal this afternoon."

"No. I did not know," Vito said sullenly.

Wayne shrugged. "All I want is an address where I can contact him."

Vito blinked his eyes rapidly. This Morgan Wayne! There had been rumors around the city for some time about a mysterious stranger from the West or someplace, and about a stupendous deal that Hake Derr was organizing to sew up the raw drug business in Manhattan with some improbably huge source of supply that would mean much money to everyone involved. This Wayne was bad, all right. He was mean and tough and soulless. The Barber, who had hummed happily in the past while he drew a razor neatly across the throats of men he had never seen before, men who had never done him any personal harm whatsoever, this same Barber now stood aghast at the spectacle of a monster in human form coolly biting off the head of one of his beloved goldfish and chewing it up and swallowing it with apparent gusto.

Nothing on earth that Wayne could have said or done could so surely have convinced Vito Saietta that Morgan Wayne was not a man to cross. He shrugged his shoulders now and said, "I will have to telephone."

Wayne said, "Go ahead."

He followed Vito across the room to the telephone, watched while he dialed a number, and listened while he said, "This is The Barber. Hake there?"

He bent his head close to Vito's and The Barber obligingly held the receiver away so both could hear the answer: "Nope. Left word he'd be at the White Star till midnight."

Vito replaced the receiver carefully. "The White Star

Club is on West Forty-ninth." He gave a street address.

Wayne nodded woodenly. He knew Vito's type. Knew exactly what The Barber was thinking. That as soon as Wayne left, Vito would call the White Star Club to warn Derr that Morgan Wayne was on his way over. Always playing both ends against the middle. Always coppering every bet. That was Vito's way.

Tonight, Morgan Wayne was playing both ends against the middle also. There was one driving compulsion inside him that overshadowed everything else. In a sense, Vito had been correct when he thought of Wayne as a monster in human form. At this moment, he was no longer human. He was a *thing*, driven by a force over which he had no control.

He drew a gun and shot Vito Saietta through the head. He pocketed the gun and walked out to continue his search for Lois' murderer.

Chapter Fifteen

WAYNE found a parking space on Forty-ninth west of Eighth Avenue and slid the Hudson into it. He sat for a moment behind the wheel, then shrugged and reached inside both jacket pockets to lift out the guns reposing there. He opened the glove compartment and shoved them inside. He had a hunch the White Star Club would be one of Hake's regular hangouts, probably one of the stations from which he conducted his sordid business, and the chances were a thousand to one that he would be well covered in a place like that.

There would be no bulling his way in as had been successful at the Gingham Gardens. Wayne was perfectly willing to take chances, but right now he wanted to stay alive until he had a chance to meet Hake Derr face to face. And walking into the White Star and asking for Hake with a couple of guns on him might not be the best way to ensure longevity.

He got out and walked briskly up the street toward a neon sign that spelled out "White Star." It was a long, low barroom typical of the neighborhood. The air was thick with smoke and the smell of stale beer and spilled liquor, mingled with the stink of sweating, unwashed bodies.

There was a juke box blaring loudly, and the dozen or more customers at the bar were half shouting at each other to be heard over it. It was an ordinary-looking West Side crowd, Wayne thought to himself as he paused inside the door to look them over. Nothing at all to distinguish the joint from any one of dozens within a few blocks—except for the two men who sat together at a table in the back of the room.

They were different from the hangers-on at the bar.

They had highball glasses in front of them, but they weren't drinking. They appeared to be lounging there at ease, but there was a hard-eyed alertness about them that belied that appearance. Pals of the two sex-crazed lice who had been holding Letty captive that afternoon, Wayne surmised after one searching glance, and he let himself wonder idly for a moment if the one whom he'd left behind with a broken jaw had come around enough to give his buddies a description of Letty's rescuer. If so, Wayne was grimly aware that it was quite possible he wouldn't stay alive long enough to have his talk with Derr. But that was one of the calculated risks he had to take.

He moved slowly down the length of the bar to an open space at the end and said, "Whisky," when he got a glance from the bartender.

When the shot glass was shoved in front of him, he asked, "Hake in back?"

The bartender was middle-aged and cherubic, with two gold teeth in front. He said, "Whyn't you ask the boys?" and took the half dollar Wayne laid beside his drink.

Morgan Wayne drank the whisky at a gulp and walked to the back. Neither of them seated at the table moved as he approached. They looked at him and waited.

He stopped beside their table and asked, "Hake busy right now?"

One of the men yawned. The other one asked, "Who wants tuh know?"

Their attitude was neither friendly nor unfriendly. It was guarded and impersonal. It was evident that they, at least, did not connect this well-dressed stranger with what had happened to Al and Charlie that afternoon.

Wayne hesitated only momentarily. This was it. He had to guess and guess right if he was to get in to see Hake Derr. He said, "Morgan Wayne."

"Huh?" The one who was yawning stopped suddenly.

His eyes narrowed and he told his companion, "That's the guy Hake said—"

"Shut up." The other got to his feet without change of expression. He opened a door to the rear and went through it, pulling it shut behind him. Wayne stood negligently beside the table and got out a pack of cigarettes. He shook one loose and politely offered it to the remaining man. He shook his head without speaking. His mouth hung open a trifle and he stared at Wayne with intense concentration. You could almost hear the cells of his mind clicking as he strove ineffectually to add two and two.

The door opened and the other man came out. He left the door open on a short corridor and said briskly to his companion, "We frisk him. Then if he's clean he goes in." He jerked his head at Wayne. "If you don't like that, the three of us go for a little ride."

"I like it," Wayne assured him, "fine."

He went through the open door and the two men followed him and pulled it shut. He turned and lifted his arms straight out from his sides and waited.

"Not that way, Bud. Strip. Right down to the skin."

Wayne smiled easily and shrugged out of his coat. "Hake must' be worried about something."

Neither man replied. They stolidly went about the task of shaking out and examining each article of clothing as Wayne removed it and handed it to them. They weren't satisfied with the outer garments, but demanded that he remove underwear, shoes, and socks also. Wayne had a derisive grin on his lips as he stood before them stark naked. "Do I go in like this?"

He intended it for a pleasantry, but neither man smiled. The one who had gone in first said, "That's it, Bud. Your clothes'll be right here when you come out." He jerked a thumb down the hall toward a door on the right that stood ajar with light streaming out. "Right in there."

There is a feeling of utter defenselessness about complete nudity. Although one knows consciously that ordinary clothing gives no protection against a lethal weapon, there is an unreasoning and panicky sense of vulnerability that accompanies nakedness.

So Hake Derr wasn't taking any chances this time, Wayne told himself grimly as he gritted his teeth and forced himself to move down the hall on bare feet to the partly open door. Well, he'd asked for this, and now he wasn't going to complain. He pushed the door open and stepped inside.

It was a large and comfortably furnished office. A fluorescent ceiling fixture flooded the room with brilliant light. A wide, flat-topped desk stood in the center of the room and Hake Derr sat in a swivel chair behind it facing the door. There was a litter of papers at his right hand, a whisky bottle and small glass at his left. He was leaning back in his chair with both hands clasped together behind his neck and a look of pleased expectation on his smooth chubby features. The cleft in his chin was very pronounced in this posture, and his round, whitish eyes didn't protrude as much as normally. Looking at him, you had a feeling he had spent hours posing before a mirror to perfect just this attitude.

It was the first time Wayne had set eyes on Hake Derr. He had heard the racketeer described, but no description had ever done him justice. Two thoughts flitted through his mind with his first look at Hake. First, that here was Priscilla Endicott's lover. And second, that here was the man who had defaced Lois Elling with a sharp knife just a few hours ago.

The two thoughts swiftly following each other contracted his hard belly muscles and brought a faint mist of red over his eyes. He controlled himself with an effort and said, "I got your message."

Derr's face smiled. "So you came looking for me."

There was a comfortable upholstered chair across the

room beyond the desk. Wayne crossed to it with as much dignity as his nakedness allowed and sat down. He said gravely, "You could have sent the same message some other way."

"But I enjoyed it that way." A light flickered evilly in the depths of the protruding gray eyes. The tip of his tongue came out to lick his thick lips with sensuous pleasure.

The man was mad. Wayne realized this with a shudder of horror as he listened to the purring voice. Mad on this one particular subject, at least. Coldly sane on all other counts, perhaps. He wondered fleetingly what form Derr's perverted pleasure would take with a man at his mercy. A naked man trapped here in his private office with not one chance in a million of escaping alive. He thrust the fleeting thought aside and made his voice angry:

"There's only one thing I want to know now. How did you know where to find her—that she was expecting me tonight?"

"That secretary of yours? Why do you care now?"

"Why shouldn't I care?" Wayne demanded hotly.

"Because you're not going to live long enough for it to matter." Derr unclasped his hands from behind his thick neck and sat forward a trifle. He laid his right hand, palm upward, on the desk and displayed a four-inch clasp knife with a single blade that sprang open in his hand as he thumbed a knob in the handle. "My God, Morgan Wayne," he asked wonderingly, "what kind of a fool are you? You know by this time that Hake Derr plays for keeps."

Wayne said wearily, "Maybe I don't want to go on living in the same world with a man like you."

"Maybe not," said Derr indifferently. "So we'll fix that easy." He was snapping the spring blade of the knife back and forth idly in his plump hand, seemingly fascinated by the play of light on the shining blade. "If you got any different ideas," he went on without bothering to look at Wayne, "get rid of them fast. I still don't know what kind of play you thought you were making by coming here to get it, but I couldn't have asked for anything better."

"So I'm here," Wayne agreed. "And I asked you a question. Who put you onto Lois Elling?"

"I got pipe lines." Derr waved his left hand.

"Is that why you didn't take Letty Hendrixon straight to the boat this afternoon—because you know it's being watched day and night?"

Derr appeared genuinely surprised. "What the hell would you do a thing like that for? What's your game, anyhow? I don't get any of this stuff you're pulling. Near as I can learn, you're not a cop, but you're not in the racket neither." He shook his head in perplexity.

Morgan Wayne had what he wanted now. What he had come for. Hake Derr didn't know about the improvised office overlooking the yacht basin.

He said pleasantly, "You'll never be able to understand this, Derr, but since you're going to kill me anyway, let me try to put it to you the best I can. You know how some people have a phobia about snakes? Just can't stand even the sight of them. They go sort of crazy and smash hell out of even an innocent little garter snake if it gets close to them."

"Sure." Derr looked baffled but interested. "I don't mind snakes myself, but I'm like that about rats. They give me the jimmies, honest to God. Even a damn little mouse."

"I happen to feel that way about human rats," Wayne said evenly. "My God, even sitting and talking to one like this makes me so sick to my stomach that I need a drink to wash the taste of it out of my mouth."

He stood up suddenly and Hake Derr shoved back his chair in sudden alarm, only dimly comprehending what Wayne was telling him, but instinctively putting a

·couple of more feet between himself and the harsh-voiced man who had suddenly come to life in his office.

"You won't begrudge me that, will you?" Wayne laughed as he reached for the whisky bottle. "One long slug of your whisky before you get started on the messy kind of killing you enjoy so much."

He caught up the open bottle near the base and with a swift motion whirled it so that hundred-proof bourbon spurted out and into Derr's face and eyes. He continued the swing downward as Derr sputtered and dabbed at his blinded eyes for one fatal instant, slamming the neck of the bottle against the sharp edge of the desk and cracking it off so a jagged half remained clutched in his hand.

He lunged forward with the saw-toothed weapon outthrust, rammed the splintered edges viciously into Hake Derr's face, and twisted as he rammed.

There was one faint, inarticulate gurgle as Derr died horribly with the flesh of his face in shreds and red blood gushing from the pierced jugular vein.

Morgan Wayne stood over him breathing heavily with the bottle still gripped in his hand and Derr's blood dripping from it down onto the faceless thing on the floor.

Then he dropped the bottle and walked unhurriedly out of the office.

The door to the barroom was closed and his clothes lay in a heap in front of it. He dressed swiftly but calmly, then turned the knob and opened the door. He turned back and hesitated as he was halfway through the opening, and called over his shoulder:

"O.K. then. Ten o'clock tomorrow."

The pair of watchdogs were seated at the same table near the door, and they watched him curiously as he stepped out and closed the door firmly behind him. It was the first time a man had ever been ushered stark naked into Hake Derr's presence and come out alive, but there was something queer about this whole Morgan Wayne business that they didn't quite grasp, and they certainly had no reason to interfere with his departure after hearing him make a date with the boss for ten o'clock next morning. Maybe there was something in the rumors going around the city that Hake was on a hell of a big deal that meant cutting in with someone else. Maybe that someone else was Morgan Wayne. He had the look of a man who knew exactly where he was going and how to get there.

He certainly had that look about him as he nodded curtly to the two watching men and strode out of the barroom.

Yet nothing was further from the truth. At the moment, Morgan Wayne hadn't the slightest idea where he was going now, or the foggiest notion of how to get there.

Indeed, as he went down the street to his parked car, he suddenly realized he didn't even know where he was going to spend the night.

Chapter Sixteen

ONE THING Morgan Wayne did know as he gunned the Hudson away from the vicinity of the White Star was that he hadn't had a single drink or a bite to eat all evening. He hadn't thought about the lack until now, but suddenly he wanted a lot of drinks and a lot of food above everything else. He looked at his wrist watch and noted with intense surprise that it was only a few minutes after ten o'clock. He couldn't recall consciously noting the time previously, and realized now that he had been going along with a vague idea that it was hours later than that.

Only six hours ago, the telephone had rung in his office for the first time since it was installed. It was incredible that so much could have happened in those six hours. Now Hake Derr was finished and he could relax. Lois Elling was avenged, though the police would never know it.

He had headed uptown after pulling away from the curb at Forty-ninth, and now a traffic light stopped him at Fifty-fourth. He remembered a small restaurant on East Fifty-fourth that catered to after-theatre patrons and served superlative drinks with the sort of good plain food that he wanted right now. It would be very lightly patronized at this hour, and Wayne turned eastward to look for it, resolutely shutting every other thought from his mind as he drove, concentrating pleasurably on the aroma and taste of a very cold and very dry Martini, and on deciding between a large sirloin steak or a thick slice of blood-red roast beef, which was a specialty of Heath House.

He had decided on roast beef by the time he crossed Madison and began looking for a parking space. With creamed white onions and a baked Idaho potato, he thought, and coffee with brandy to top it off.

He was greeted at the door by a smiling headwaiter who did not know him by name but recalled the generous tips he had left on previous visits. Only half a dozen tables were occupied, as Wayne had expected, and he was immediately seated in a corner with a waiter hovering expectantly.

"I need drinks," Wayne said succinctly. "Martinis as cold as a banker's handclasp and as dry as a deacon's cupboard. Half a dozen of them, probably. Just watch my glass and keep them coming. And tip the chef off to reserve me his bloodiest slice of beef."

He grimaced slightly as the words left his mouth, but the waiter noticed nothing and hurried beamingly away to bring the first cocktail. Wayne wondered idly how the waiter would react if he explained to him why he grimaced over the mention of blood aloud; if he described how Hake Derr's face had looked on the floor at his feet only fifteen minutes ago. He felt enervated, now that it was over, and slightly listless. He had been keyed up for too many hours, of course. There had to be a letdown.

He lifted the Martini eagerly when it came, sipped appreciatively, and then gulped half the glass. He nodded to the waiter, who had remained for his approval, and said, "I'll be ready for another by the time you can get it here."

The first drink did wonders for him. He drank the second one slowly, as a truly good cocktail should be taken, and let his thoughts move ahead to the problem of what his next step should be.

The killing of Hake Derr ended one phase of the affair, but only one phase. Derr had been an important cog in the plot to seize control of Durtol Drugs by the underworld, but only a cog. His death was not likely materially to disrupt the careful plan. There would be another man ready to step into Derr's shoes at once, and Operation Durtol would proceed as scheduled.

The wiping out of rats like The Barber and Hake Derr wasn't the real answer. One had to get to the top to accomplish anything worth while in the struggle against the insidious forces whose slimy tentacles were becoming more numerous and powerful every day.

Wayne had realized this from the very first when he had decided to throw himself into the struggle. This was why he had made no previous attempt to come to grips with Derr or any of his minions. He had watched and waited patiently, hoping for a break that would give him a lead to the man who was the real brains behind the boldly planned coup.

Until tonight. Until the wanton murder of his secretary had unleased forces within him that would brook no further delay.

Perhaps it had been a mistake in tactics to go after Derr, Wayne admitted somberly to himself as he finished his third drink. So be it. It had been inevitable from the moment he discovered Lois' body and knew who her killer was. He refused to regret what he had done. But now it was over, and he would have to turn himself back into the coldly reasoning and remorselessly logical machine he had been before Lois' death.

The cocktails helped. They cleared away the fog and clarified the situation as it now stood. He did have one lead, he reminded himself grimly. There could be no hesitancy about following it through. The time to strike was now. While Derr's death caused at least a slight interruption in the smooth functioning of the plan.

The real answer, he now knew, lay in the Hendrixon household itself. He had begun to suspect the truth earlier in the evening, but now he knew without a shadow of a doubt that Lois had been betrayed to her death by one of the persons who knew about her telephone call to Julius Hendrixon.

It had to be that way. No matter *what* the Gingham Girl really was. No matter how jealous she had been or how strongly she might have desired Lois' death, Wayne now knew that she hadn't possessed the necessary information to have sent Hake Derr to Lois' apartment. Though she admitted telling Hake that Morgan Wayne had a date with his secretary, that alone had not been enough. There wasn't a shadow of doubt in Wayne's mind that Derr's surprise had been genuine when he denied knowing that Wayne had been keeping a close watch on his docked yacht for weeks. Which was proof that Derr was not aware of the existence of the improvised office overlooking the yacht basin, and thus could not possibly have known the identity of Wayne's secretary.

So Priscilla's tip-off would not have been enough. The information about Lois must have come from another source. And probably the order to dispose of her also, Wayne went on grimly with his reasoning. He was sipping his fifth cocktail now, and his mind was working with clockwork precision. It wasn't the sort of move that would occur to a mentality like Derr's, though it was certain he would have welcomed the suggestion that he strike at Wayne through an unsuspecting and defenseless girl. That assignment would have been right up Hake Derr's alley and he would have accepted it with enthusiasm.

And the thought of Lois' defenselessness as she waited for him in her black negligee was the clincher in Wayne's line of reasoning. Rat-souled killer that he was, Derr would have hesitated to go to Lois' apartment on his deadly errand unless he were assured that she would be alone—and that he could not possibly be interrupted by Wayne before the job was done and he could slink out.

To be assured of that, he must have known exactly what time Wayne left the Hendrixon mansion to drive into the city. Only those persons present when Wayne left could have given Derr the needed information.

Julius and his wife and his wife's brother . . . and Attorney Carson. Only those four knew the time he left the house, *and also knew about his appointment with Lois Elling.* Only one of those four could have communicated with Derr by telephone to send him on his deadly errand.

It made sense, of course. From the very first, Wayne had realized that the coup must certainly have been planned and was being engineered by someone close to the Durtol Drug empire and in a position to profit by the wholesale switching of legal drugs to illicit markets.

But this night's work narrowed it down tremendously.

Julius Hendrixon, John Durtol III, Mrs. Hendrixon, Elliot Carson.

One of those four. Two of them the parents of the young girl whose kidnaping had been arranged to press the plan through. And her uncle. And the trusted attorney and family friend.

Morgan Wayne nodded pleasantly to the waiter when his sixth cocktail was placed in front of him. "You can tell the chef to go to work now. A large baked potato, creamed onions, and a tossed salad. With your special roquefort dressing."

Yes. One of those four. One of them had got to a telephone soon after Wayne left the house and communicated with Hake Derr. One who had been frightened by Wayne's knowledge of the plot to seize control of Durtol Drugs, and who had been fool enough to think the simplest and safest way to discourage him from further investigation was to murder the woman with whom he had a date and leave the warning for him to "lay off."

Which one? None of them outwardly seemed to fit the role, yet Wayne had a queasy feeling that each one of the four was a distinct possibility.

Even Letty's mother?

Yes, goddamn it! he told himself savagely. Even Letty's mother. There was something about her that gave him that feeling. Despite the scene Mrs. Hendrixon had put on when her daughter was returned, Wayne had a hunch she was just about as maternal as a sow who has to be forcibly restrained from eating her litter as soon as it's born.

Actually, Carson was first on his list of suspects. Not a member of the family and thus wholly without sentimental attachment to the honor and reputation of Durtol Drugs, but still in a position to pull strings and manipulate the management to make the coup successful.

In fact, as his food came and Wayne attacked it with hearty appetite, he found himself wondering if it weren't very possible that Julius Hendrixon was merely a figurehead for Carson—if the lawyer had not contrived to have him put in charge of the firm's affairs so that he would have a ready tool to be manipulated at the right time.

Certainly, Julius had appeared something of an ass on their first meeting a month previously when he had laughed at Wayne's warning and disregarded it, and again tonight. Hardly the high type of successful business executive one expected to find at the helm of an enterprise like Durtol Drugs. You couldn't be sure, of course. His rough exterior and coarse manner might conceal an intelligence of the highest order. It was no use jumping to conclusions based on such brief acquaintanceship with the four persons involved.

Deductions were no good at this point. Some sort of concrete proof was needed. It might be possible to narrow the field of conjecture if he could learn which one or ones of the quartet had had access to a private telephone soon after he left the house. He was positive in his own mind that one of them had telephoned Derr to order the death of Lois. If it were possible to prove that one or more of them could *not* have made such a call, they could be eliminated from consideration.

Well, he had one pipe line into the Hendrixon household that none of them knew about, Wayne reminded himself wryly. He didn't particularly relish getting mixed up any further with Letty's adolescent fevers. But he *had* promised her they would be alone together. A promise was a promise, he told himself sternly. Of course, when he gave it to her it had been with the mental reservation that it might be years before he kept it.

But now he knew it couldn't be years. Or even months or weeks. It would have to be at once. Tomorrow, if possible. While the events of tonight were fresh in her mind and he might be able to get a coherent account of the movements of each of the four people involved immediately after his departure.

He was pleasantly relaxed with his coffee, a pony of superb Napoleon brandy, and a cigarette when he suddenly recalled that he still didn't know where he would spend the night. The apartment to which he had taken Letty was out of the question. It would be closely watched by the police and he didn't relish the idea of being hauled into a precinct station and being held there for hours, perhaps, until he could establish contact with some official high enough in the Department to vouch for him and order his release.

There was the Gingham Gardens—and Priscilla.

His heart began to pound at the thought of going to her and explaining that she need fear no further interference from Hake Derr. But he didn't know. He didn't yet know where Priscilla fitted into the picture. If her liaison with Derr had been prompted purely and simply by selfish mercenary reasons, as she claimed, then that cleared her of any complicity in the drug racket or murder, but was, nonetheless, quite distasteful to Wayne. As he thought about her now, he wanted her again with every fiber of his strong body, but he was romanticist enough to desire fiercely more than merely a body that was for sale to the highest bidder. Perhaps he was a fool to want more. Often in the past, it hadn't made any difference. But with Priscilla, it did. There had been something about her when he first looked at her. Something he didn't want to laugh at, or to forget.

No. He knew he couldn't go to Priscilla's bed until the situation and her place in it had been resolved one way or another. Either way would suffice. If he were once convinced that she had nothing but an evilly beautiful and wantonly debauched body to offer him, he knew he would gladly take that and do with it what she wanted him to do. But not until he was convinced there could be nothing more for him from Priscilla Endicott.

He thought about Letty Hendrixon again, and grimaced when he found himself studying his watch speculatively.

Almost eleven. And it was practically an hour's drive to her house. Much too late to go calling now. Not because Letty wouldn't welcome him, but because it would probably be impossible to see her without others knowing.

Still, it might not be too late to telephone and ask about her condition after the trying events of the day. Tell her good night, perhaps, and suggest a meeting for tomorrow.

Wayne lifted a finger at his waiter and asked for a telephone to be plugged in. He called the Hendrixon number and heard the phone ring twice. Then a woman's voice said, "Mrs. Hendrixon's residence."

The housekeeper, he thought, or a maid. He said, "May I speak to Mrs. Hendrixon, please?"

"Madame has retired and I am afraid that will be impossible tonight."

Wayne thought he heard the faint click of another receiver coming off the hook, and he said smoothly, "I understand. Will you please tell her that Morgan Wayne called, and—"

"I'll take it, Jessica. You can hang up. Morgy!" It was

Letty's eager young voice trilling over the wire. As fresh and effervescent as though she had just wakened and showered after ten hours' sleep.

"I just knew you'd call," she went on as soon as the other receiver clicked. "How soon can you get here? Where are you now?"

"I'm in town." Wayne hesitated and adopted a fatherly tone. "What you need is bed. If you can get away tomorrow—"

"What I need is you in bed with me." Letty chuckled with delight at what she considered the shameless sophistication of her remark, and went on swiftly, "You needn't be frightened. It's perfectly safe. Everyone else is sound asleep except me and I've just been waiting for you to call. Don't turn in the front drive when you come," she went on before he could protest. "Drive right past about two hundred yards and park. There's a path leading up to the gardener's cottage, only it's vacant now, and I'll be waiting for you there. It'll be dark because the electricity is cut off, but you can't miss it. I'll be waiting for you, Morgy." She hung up.

Wayne hesitated with the receiver to his ear. While she had been speaking so swiftly to forestall any argument from him, he thought he had heard the sound of another receiver being very cautiously lifted on the line. He wondered how many extensions there were in the house, and whether it had merely been a curious servant or someone else. To be sure he had not imagined the sound, he said, "Wait, Letty. Are you still there?"

He waited and there was no sound. Then he simulated a groan and flipped a fingernail against the mouthpiece. It made a very satisfactory click, and almost immediately he heard another receiver being replaced on the other end.

He hung up and considered the situation wryly. Letty would be waiting at the gardener's cottage when he arrived—*if* he arrived—he had no doubt of that.

But who else would be waiting also?

He shrugged fatalistically as he called for his check. Perhaps it was just as well. It might force a showdown of sorts. Anything he could learn about the Hendrixon menage might be the one thing he needed. Any sort of action was better than sitting around twiddling his fingers. Even a midnight date with Letty—with the distinct possibility of being spied upon by either or both of her parents.

In fact, it was this possibility that decided Wayne to keep the date Letty had made. No matter how irresponsible they were as parents, he thought he could depend on either of them to interfere and break things up before they went too far. Without that assurance he would not have cared to tackle an assignation with the precocious Letty.

Chapter Seventeen

THERE were no policemen stationed at the Hendrixon turnoff this time, no lights showing from the big house on the hill as Wayne drove slowly past.

There was a bright moon overhead, partially obscured by fleecy white clouds, and Wayne leaned out the window to watch carefully for the path through the woods that Letty had mentioned over the telephone.

He found it about two hundred yards beyond the driveway as she had said, and pulled to the side to cut ignition and lights.

There was no sound as he got out of the car and stood there for a moment wondering how many kinds of fool a man could be, after all. Not even the faint night sounds that one expects in the country. Not the slightest breeze to rustle the leaves of the trees, no crickets or frogs to greet him as he climbed the path. He expected, actually, to be accosted at any moment. Even if it had been a servant listening in on the last part of the conversation, he believed a servant would have certainly informed master or mistress about Letty's arrangement of a midnight tryst in the gardener's cottage.

He hadn't planned what he would say if he was accosted. That would have to depend on circumstances, on who did the accosting and what sort of story Letty had told to explain how she happened to know Morgan Wayne well enough to be willing to meet him like this.

Whatever story Letty told, Wayne thought to himself that it would be a good one. He would try to follow through as best he could. At least this was action. And it would bring forth some sort of reaction.

The upward path was narrow and winding through the underbrush, and there was short grass underfoot that deadened the sound of his steps. He continued to move doggedly upward, and eventually come out into a small moonlit clearing with a clapboard cottage in the center of it.

Morgan Wayne paused in the last bit of shadow and listened intently before stepping into the moonlight. The cottage stood dark and silent in front of him. Over his left shoulder he could see the dark hulk of the Hendrixon mansion without a light showing. So far as any outward signs went, he was the only person awake in all of Westchester County.

He drew in a deep breath and dropped both hands into his coat pockets and stepped boldly out into the moonlight toward the silent cottage.

He reached the front door without incident. Every sense was alert and every nerve on edge as he turned the doorknob and pushed. The door opened easily and soundlessly. He moved with it swiftly, over the threshold and a step aside to press his back against the wall and avoid being silhouetted in the opening for anyone who might be waiting inside.

Still nothing happened. Faint moonlight came through the open door at his left and touched a few objects in the room. An upholstered chair standing near the door, a small round table a little beyond. The rest of the room was in darkness.

He held his breath for a long moment and listened intently, closing his eyes to adjust them more quickly to the dark. Blood drummed loudly in his ears and he could hear no other sound. But there was an intangible *feel* of some other living being close to him. An odor, perhaps, or an other-worldly emanation that touched off some sixth sense he didn't know he possessed.

He opened his eyes and said quietly, "Where are you, Letty?"

Then he saw her. The tenuous and shimmering whiteness of flesh standing erect not more than ten feet from him. The figure did not move and it didn't speak. It was ghostlike and unreal.

Wayne said angrily, "Why don't you say something, Letty? It's Morgan Wayne." He moved toward her.

She waited for him to come. Without moving and without speaking. When he had covered half the distance he was conscious of the smell of her body. The thing he had sensed on first entering without being quite aware what it was.

The figure became less ghostlike and more real. There were two white limbs and a white torso and white arms outstretched to enfold him in her embrace. It was like Letty to put on a show like this, he thought with irrational anger as he neared her. She must have read in some book that women should be mysterious and silently alluring. He said indulgently, "Relax, for God's sake, before I turn you over my knee and—"

She surged forward against him and her hot arms were around his neck before he could avoid the embrace. She pressed her body against him and pressed her mouth on his, clinging fiercely about his neck with surprising strength. His hands went behind her back instinctively, and he found it sinewy and strong, the flesh firm and fever-hot beneath his hands.

It all happened in seconds, and it was seconds more before Wayne's dazed comprehension told him this was no naïve adolescent hungering for her first lesson in sex. This was a mature and lustful woman, crazed with desire and with waiting in the night for a man to come to her. She was moaning queerly now, gasping obscene phrases, struggling with all her strength to pull him off his feet so they would go to the floor together.

From an indulgent determination to fight off Letty's youthful advances, Wayne's mood swiftly changed to one of answering passion. He had no time to question who she was or why she waited here in Letty's place. He was confronted in the darkness with a woman whose ardor aroused his own and his arms tightened about her and he staggered forward two steps to the dim outline of a couch against the wall.

She squirmed beneath him as they fell, the fingers of one hand twined savagely in his hair.

When at last she sank back, limp and exhausted, Wayne lifted himself on both elbows to stare down at the white oval of her face beneath his.

It was Mrs. Hendrixon. Letty's mother. Her eyes were closed and her lips parted to let her spent breath in and out.

Morgan Wayne closed his eyes and counted to ten slowly. He had expected anything but this. Some sex-starved housemaid, perhaps, or an older contemporary of Letty's who had somehow arranged to pinch-hit for her in this midnight adventure.

But the woman who had assaulted him so savagely was Mrs. Julius Hendrixon.

Wayne rolled over on his side and fumbled in his pocket for a cigarette. He was a fool to be surprised, he told himself moodily. There had been warning enough in those vagrant glances he had caught from her earlier in the evening. And Letty herself had hinted something of this to him.

He snapped his lighter and put flame to his cigarette, and she opened her eyes to smile dreamily up at him. She was almost beautiful in her blissful state of contentment. Her features were softened, her eyes moist and warm, her nostrils wide at the base and quivering under his eyes. She asked huskily, "Could I have a cigarette, please?"

Wayne got out a cigarette and inserted it between her parted lips. Her eyelids came down as he thumbed his lighter again. She drew smoke deep into her lungs and murmured, "Thanks."

"For the cigarette?"

"For everything. You're . . . what I knew you'd be."

"You're not," he told her bluntly.

The burning tip of her cigarette flared as she sucked in smoke again. Her lips were smiling. "Disappointed that I'm not Letty?"

"God, no! Just trying to believe you are you."

She yawned and stretched sinuously. "Am I really better than she?"

The question came eagerly, with no maternal overtones whatever.

"I never experimented with Letty," Wayne told her shortly. "Frankly, I like my women a few years above the age of consent."

She said thoughtfully, "I wonder if Letty still is a virgin."

"Not if she's been able to find any man to give her what she wants."

She laughed without constraint. "She's always been that way." She stretched voluptuously again. "How did she come to pick on you, darling?"

"Because I wear pants. What does she think about your substituting for her?"

"Heavens, she doesn't know anything about it. Poor lamb, she's peacefully asleep. She'll be *so* disappointed when she wakens tomorrow."

"Do you mean she just dropped off to sleep after talking to me on the phone?" demanded Wayne incredulously, his male vanity touched.

"After drinking a glass of warm milk I thoughtfully provided, with six sleeping tablets dissolved in it." She stubbed her cigarette out against the wall beside her and reached for him with avid fingers. "We're wasting time talking about Letty."

This time it was not so tempestuous, but actually more violent in the end. Wayne understood the sort of woman she was and the sort of thing she had to have. He was not loath to oblige her. There is a deep-rooted instinct in every virile male that responds savagely to such desires in a woman. She was weak with exhaustion when they lighted second cigarettes.

Morgan Wayne lay beside her in the darkness and muttered, "It's like questioning a gift of the gods, but I still can't understand why the wife of a man like Julius Hendrixon is lying out here with me."

"Julius?" There was scorn and loathing in her voice. "He's about as much good to a woman as a hatrack."

"That hulk of man?" Wayne was honestly surprised. "He looks like the sort who could keep a harem happy."

"It's all on the outside," she said bitterly. "I thought so, too, five years ago, when I married him. Why else would I marry a boor like that?" she went on angrily. "A nobody with nothing to his name. So little Harriet fell for his uncouth manners and brawny frame. I could have had the pick of hundreds, and I end up with him." She laughed stridently. "He didn't want me. He wanted my money. Management of the company and power. Durtol Drugs is his real wife. He has no time to spare for me."

Wayne sucked on his cigarette and let her talk. So she and Julius had been married only five years, and he was actually Letty's stepfather. A man who was greedy for money and for power.

Wayne sighed with deep satisfaction. If he could keep Julius' thwarted wife talking long enough, he might get everything he needed without moving from the couch beside her.

"How's Carson for a bedmate?" he asked casually.

"What makes you think I'd know?" She was instantly on her guard.

Wayne said negligently, "I thought I noticed he had a roving eye tonight. Don't try to pull a prudish act on me," he went on with a laugh. "You didn't let any grass grow under your feet before undressing for me."

"You're different." She reached out in the darkness to take hold of his hand and squeeze it. "But why should I be prudish? Elliot's an old darling, but he's *old*. Fifty at least. He *had* half promised to stay and see me tonight after Julius went to bed, if you must know."

"And then stood you up?" Wayne asked with amusement.

"He left for the city right after you did, without saying a word. But I'm glad now that he did."

So that's one, Wayne told himself. One of the four who could easily have got to a telephone to call Hake Derr. He asked disinterestedly, "What did your husband and brother do?"

"Sat around talking a while, I guess. Then John went home and Julius came up and had a couple of drinks in my sitting room."

"Are you sure he's asleep now? Durtol Drugs may be his mistress," Wayne went on with a laugh, "but I still don't take him for the sort of man who'd wear a pair of horns without objecting rather strenuously."

"You needn't worry about him." She squeezed Wayne's hand comfortingly. "He hadn't got to bed when Elliot phoned him from the city to meet him at once on some mysterious business. Something about Letty's kidnaping this afternoon, I gathered, though he didn't say so outright."

"When was that?"

"About an hour and a half ago. Just a little before you telephoned Letty. Let's talk about us." Her voice became languidly amorous. "How are we going to meet in the future? Don't spoil everything by telling me you have an insanely jealous wife whom you love dearly."

He managed a light laugh. "No wife," he assured her. "No encumbrances at all. I can't help wondering about your brother," he went on hurriedly. "Didn't he resent it when you married Julius and brought him in to manage the business that was John's responsibility by direct inheritance?"

"Resent it? Lord, no. John is much happier than I with the arrangement. He has all the time in the world now for his showgirls and gambling, and lots more money to spend on them since Julius took over the reins, and dividends have gone up every year."

"Are we talking about the same person?" asked Wayne dubiously. "Showgirls and gambling don't sound like John's forte."

"He's a complete wastrel," she assured him complacently. "He cultivates that indolent, gentlemanly air just for effect." She turned and pressed her mouth against his, pulled him to her again in the darkness, demanding, "*Why* are we wasting all this time, lover?"

Chapter Eighteen

WHEN Morgan Wayne left the gardener's cottage on the Hendrixon estate, he had the address of John Durtol III and a fervid promise from Mrs. Hendrixon to meet him again any time and any place he selected.

The first item was important to him, but he felt he could get along very well without the second. A woman like Harriet Hendrixon was wonderful for a one-night stand, but she was likely to become dynamite if a man kept on with her. A frustrated woman of her age, with no inhibitions to slow her down, was likely to lose all sense of proportion and throw herself into an affair with no thought whatsoever of any possible consequences.

But she had served him one good turn tonight, Wayne reminded himself wryly as he went down the path to his parked car. She'd got Letty off his neck, and the girl wouldn't have any reason to come around in the future to remind him of his promise. *He* hadn't broken it, he would point out to Letty. *He* had kept the tryst, and she was the one who had disappointed him. He grinned as he thought about her waking up in the morning, dopey from the effects of six sleeping pills and wondering what on earth had possessed her to drop off to sleep instead of going out to the cottage to meet him. Give her a few more years, he thought indulgently, and she'd be another nymphomaniac like her mother. Then it might be worth while looking her up again. Another edition of Harriet Hendrixon and half her age would be worth investigating sometime in the future.

Characteristically, Morgan Wayne abruptly wiped all thought of the female members of the Hendrixon clan from his mind as he got in the Hudson and made a U turn back toward the city. It had been difficult to pry very much essential information from Harriet without revealing why he wanted it, but he did have several rather important bits to think about.

Julius' real character, for instance, was becoming increasingly evident. A dominant, masculine sort of man whose sexual drive had been diverted to business. A penniless nobody, Harriet had intimated, until he lured her into marriage by his outward masculinity, and achieved control of Durtol Drugs. An avaricious man, mad for power. That fitted the picture Wayne had been building up in his own mind of the person who was using Hake Derr as a tool to turn the legitimate business of the drug company into illicit channels. Everything began to fit in, once you perceived the man's true character.

In the beginning, it had appeared doubtful whether a father would cold-bloodedly arrange the kidnaping of his own daughter, but that objection was removed once one knew that Letty was actually his stepdaughter. And it was Julius' wife who actually owned the block of stock, Wayne reminded himself. It was quite possible that she couldn't be persuaded to sell in any other way. If it was Julius Hendrixon, he must have felt quite safe and clever in having his own daughter kidnaped to put pressure on his wife. No one would suspect a husband of an atrocious deed like that, and he was right on the inside where he could keep his finger on the pulse of things and warn his confederates of any moves the police were making.

This fitted in, too, with Julius' first reaction to Wayne's warning about the projected kidnaping a month ago. Of course, he would have scoffed at any such idea if he, himself, were planning it. Wayne's first visit must have given him some anxious moments, but Hake Derr would have reassured him. So far as he and Derr had known, Wayne was merely a crackpot who had got hold of a rumor somehow.

It was quite possible, Wayne thought, that Elliot Carson was in on the plan with Hendrixon. The telephone message for Julius to come to the city at midnight seemed to indicate more than an ordinary business connection between the pair. The time of Carson's call coincided roughly with the time that Derr's death had probably been discovered. That could easily account for the hurried conference ordered by the lawyer. From the description Derr's bodyguards could provide, it must have been evident to Carson that Wayne was Derr's killer—that he had *not* reacted properly to the "lay off" warning delivered to him in Lois Elling's bedroom.

John Durtol might know where the two men would be meeting. He probably wouldn't, but the young man might well possess other information that would clinch the case against his brother-in-law. Durtol's bachelor apartment was Wayne's first stop on his way into the city, and he planned to put his suspicions squarely up to Harriet's brother. He wouldn't, he thought with secret amusement, tell John where and under what circumstances he had got his information, for even the most decadent of brothers is apt to be a bit touchy about his sister's honor, but he would tell him enough to convince John that the interests of the drug firm demanded his full co-operation.

The address Harriet Hendrixon had given him was in one of the new, huge residential apartment developments that had mushroomed recently on the outskirts of the city just off the West Side Highway. With a general idea of the location in mind, Wayne had little trouble locating the Elvira Manor development, but it did take him fifteen minutes and half a dozen inquiries to find the particular wing in which Durtol's apartment was situated.

There was an air of haughty and chaste elegance about the entire setup that depressed Wayne immeasurably as he rode skyward in an elevator large enough to accom-

modate twenty persons, accompanied only by an operator whose uniform would have put a Peruvian admiral
to shame.

There was a wide, vaulted corridor when he got out of
the elevator, from which endless side passages darted off ·
in a confusing maze. Wayne plodded doggedly along on
an inch-thick carpet, consulting numbers as he went and
pausing at various crossroads to study the arrows pointing in four directions and attempt to interpret the sym-
bols in neon lights over each arrow.

He finally arrived at a heavy oak door marked 1482-X
and stopped in front of it with a sigh of relief. He put his
finger on the bell and didn't bother to take it off. It was
past one o'clock in the morning, and if John Durtol III
were at home he would certainly be asleep unless occupied in some other manner that would make him just
as disinclined to admit a late visitor.

Wayne began to think he wasn't at home after a full
sixty seconds had passed without any response to his
ringing. He frowned but kept his finger on the button.
John was his one chance to contact any of the Durtol
group at this hour, and Wayne was in a fever of impatience to keep on moving now that he had finally got
started.

After one minute and forty seconds of steady ringing
his stubbornness brought results. The knob turned and
the heavy door swung inward soundlessly.

In a small foyer lighted from floor lamps in the long
living room beyond an archway, a girl confronted him.
She was barefooted and wore a short, quilted mandarin
robe. Her hair was cut as short as a boy's and she was
rubbing her eyes sleepily with both fists and yawning
widely. She didn't actually look at Wayne as she murmured, "So you decided to come back, Johnsey?"

Wayne stepped inside, closed the door, and took her
firmly by the elbow. She dropped her knuckles from her
eyes and blinked up at him in round-faced amazement.

She had no make-up on, and looked like a frightened farm girl with her natural healthy coloring and well-fleshed features.

"Who are you?" she asked in some alarm. "Where's Johnsey?"

"I was about to ask you both questions." Wayne smiled down at her reassuringly.

She shrugged and turned away from him into the large inner room that had a ceiling two floors up and a railed balcony on three sides at the second-floor level. She curled up on a sofa with her bare legs tucked under her and yawned again before saying indifferently, "I'm Marge, and if you know much about John you won't ask me what I'm doing here. That crazy galoot. He gives me a diamond wrist watch from Tiffany's to promise to spend the night and then ducks out before we get started." The farm-girl look had gone now, but she retained the look of a healthy young animal without a trace of the sophistication Wayne would have thought John Durtol III would require in an overnight guest.

Wayne sat down across the room from her and lit a cigarette and smiled. "He's a nut, all right, if he walked out on you."

She shrugged and looked down at her broad, stubby-fingered hands. "How does he get that way," she burst out indignantly, "making a girl bring a doctor's affidavit that she's a virgin before he'll sleep with her? What kind of fun can a man get out of *that*? I ask you! All the fellows I ever knew intimate enough to ask tell me the first time isn't ever any good."

"Did you bring your affidavit?" Wayne chuckled.

"Sure I did. After I had the wrist watch appraised. Mom always told me not to sell out cheap, but I figured no one would ever offer me more than twenty thousand smackers. Don't you think I was right?"

"Right as rain," Wayne assured her gravely. "Do you know where John went?"

"That's what gets my goddamned nanny goat. That gingham bitch called him, that's what. How do you figure a guy like that?" she demanded wonderingly. "Making me bring along my certificate and then bouncing out before we even get in bed just because he gets a phone call from a floosie that hasn't had one for a cinch since she was ten years old. Hey, that reminds me of a joke," she went on vivaciously, wrinkling up her nose at Wayne.

"In Sunday school, see, and this class of kids are having a lesson from the Bible about the ten virgins or whatever. So the teacher asks the class do any of them know what a virgin is, and one little girl sticks up her hand quick and gets up and says, 'A virgin is a little girl eleven years old—no, ten years old, I mean. I'm eleven.' D'yuh get the point?" She shook with laughter, shaking her head from side to side. "She was eleven, see? And she knew a virgin was younger than *she* was."

"I get it," said Wayne patiently as soon as he could break in. "Do you mean to say by any wild and impossible chance that it was Priscilla Endicott who telephoned John and lured him away from your charms?"

"I dunno what her name is," she said sullenly. "But I know she sings in a lousy cellar joint on Fifty-second. And Johnsey goes running if she crooks her finger at him. How do you like that from a guy that passes out diamond wrist watches from Tiffany's?"

Morgan Wayne was on his way to the door before her flow of conversation ceased.

Chapter Nineteen

Morgan Wayne didn't have the faintest idea how this new bit of information fitted into the pattern, but he headed fast for Fifty-second Street when he got away from Elvira Manor.

If Marge was correct and John Durtol III was actually mixed up with the Gingham Girl, a whole new realm of interesting speculation was opened up. Was Priscilla the go-between who had brought Hake Derr into the Durtol picture? It was possible she had played the role unwittingly. It was also quite possible, Wayne assured himself grimly, that she brought the two men together purposefully. Nothing he learned about Priscilla Endicott would really surprise him. He didn't even discount the possibility that she was entangled in this affair from a motive as pure as his own; that she was using her body as a weapon to smash the drug traffic just as Wayne employed the two guns weighting down his jacket pockets.

He knew, down deep in his heart, that he hoped that explanation was true. There had been that about Priscilla Endicott when he first looked at her. She had something that made a man *want* to believe she was basically decent.

At any rate, that strong intuitive feeling he had had as he first entered the Gingham Gardens early that evening was now intensified. The key to the whole situation was there. Tonight's affair had begun in the Gingham Gardens, and he felt it would end there. If Priscilla held the key, he would wrest it from her somehow.

He wrenched his musings away from her and brought them back to John Durtol III, Julius Hendrixon, and Elliot Carson. At the moment the only visible connection between any of the three with the underworld was John's infatuation with Priscilla—if the impatient virgin at John's apartment could be relied upon. But the perplexing thing about suspecting John was the fact that he already owned enough Durtol stock to enable him to gain control by consolidating with the other blocks of stock that had already been bought up—thus leaving him no real motive for arranging Letty's kidnaping to force his sister to sell her stock.

It seemed a foolish and unnecessary risk to Morgan Wayne. The whole affair could have been handled smoothly and with no risk at all if John Durtol III were actually the moving spirit in the plan. He didn't know yet, Wayne reminded himself, that John had even been aware of Hake Derr's existence. With a woman of Priscilla's undoubted talents for intrigue involved, it was entirely possible that neither man had known the other was enjoying her favors. But what a hell of an ill-assorted pair, Wayne thought irrationally, to have been selected by Priscilla for bedmates. A ruthless killer like Derr who confessed that his greatest pleasure came from using his knife on a woman, and the seemingly spineless heir to the Durtol fortune. It was inconceivable that she should have picked those two at random from all the men in New York whom she might have had simply by crooking her finger.

Certainly, neither of them suited her temperamentally. No matter how many questions there were in Wayne's mind as to Priscilla's real nature, he had absolutely no doubt that her passionate response to him that afternoon had been honest. A vision of her came to him as he drove through the night toward her, as she had been in his arms after their first kiss. Her face peaceful and with a strange look of content. The look of little-girl pleading in her wide eyes, the surprised and almost virginal look of ecstasy. The dreamy langour of her reply when he had asked her if she wanted to die: "I don't think I care. Take me in your arms."

He drew in a great, shuddering breath as the memory came vividly to him.

No. That had been real. And it was impossible for Wayne to understand that same woman wanting either Hake Derr or John Durtol as she had wanted him that afternoon. The same woman *couldn't*. No matter how many facets there were to her nature, she couldn't give the same thing to either of those others that she had freely offered to Morgan Wayne.

So there had to be another explanation of her reasons for taking them to bed. Money? Could it be only that? That was her explanation, but the words hadn't rung true when she spoke them. That had been, of course, before he knew she was even acquainted with John Durtol III. It sounded more reasonable now that he knew. She had spoken of an impending deal that would put Derr up among the Rockefellers and the Morgans within a few years. It made a lot more sense if she were in the middle of the plot that was being engineered by Durtol and Derr. Playing ball with both of them, she might have looked on the proposition as a sure winner. And her midnight telephone call to John seemed to bear that out. With Derr's death, an immediate shifting of plans would be necessary, an immediate meeting of the remaining two principals to decide matters of policy.

Exactly the same reasoning, Wayne realized, that made the rush call from Carson to Hendrixon appear suspicious on the surface. There simply wasn't any use trying to guess at the truth at this point. If he found John Durtol III with Priscilla, he would get the truth out of the two of them. If John hadn't been there or had already gone back to Marge, he would have to work on Priscilla alone.

He had reached the nearest exit for Fifty-second Street when he arrived at the conclusion, and he forced himself to relax behind the wheel of the borrowed car as he turned eastward. It was almost two o'clock and the midtown street was practically empty of traffic. A few restaurants with late licenses still stood open, catering to the late drinkers who wouldn't leave until the final drink was poured.

Wayne didn't know whether the Gingham Gardens would be one of these or not as he approached. There was no spotlighted painting on the sidewalk to draw attention to the place, and the outer neon lights were turned off.

But as Wayne slid in to the curb directly in front, he saw a hazy glow of light emanating from the dim foyer that was down three steps from the sidewalk, and when he got out of the car the same doorman under his three-cornered headpiece of gingham strolled across the walk and repeated the same warning Wayne had heard earlier:

"No parking here, sir. You'll have to . . ."

The pattern repeated itself immutably. Wayne said pleasantly, "Watch my car, will you?" A second ten-dollar bill was swallowed up in the doorman's hand and he said, "Certainly, sir," to Wayne's back as he went down the three steps.

There was a different girl at the check stand, and Wayne remembered that the blonde had said she'd be off in a couple of hours. This one was a pert little wren with short, fluffy hair that was obviously platinumed. Unlike her predecessor, she wore a tight gingham halter over almost nonexistent breasts, showing an expanse of flat stomach to a point well below her navel, and she had an eager smile of welcome that contrasted well with the frozen, tailored quality of the blonde's.

Like the other girl's, though, her eagerness faded from her smile when she saw that Wayne was hatless. Again the pattern repeated itself, for again Wayne was after information.

He smiled reassuringly as he went toward her, and explained, "It's not that I don't like check girls—I just don't like hats." There was a folded five-dollar bill between his fingers as he leaned on her counter. She plucked it out in a matter-of-fact way and told him, "I wouldn't kick if all my customers felt that way."

Wayne said casually, "Is Johnsey around?"

"Who?" She wrinkled her snub nose as she smoothed the bill over one palm.

"Durtol. John Durtol Third." Wayne grinned engagingly as he spoke the full name. "One of the Gingham Gal's particular friends."

"Gee, I dunno, mister." She giggled maliciously. "First I heard she was particular."

Wayne nodded casually as though it didn't matter, and sauntered inside.

The long bar was crowded now, and more than half the tables were occupied. The heavy smoke haze that hung over the room made his eyes smart so it was difficut to see clearly.

Wayne didn't bother to look for Willie Sutra because he knew exactly how hard he had hit him on his last trip. There was a fast-jiving man at the piano in the rear now, and no singer at the moment. No sign of Priscilla that Wayne could see as he stood near the end of the bar and studied the occupants of the room with hooded eyes.

The same beefy bartender he had encountered on his first trip pushed in front of him on the other side of the bar and asked wearily, "What's yours, Mac?"

Wayne turned to look him full in the face, and shook his head slowly. "Just a cheapskate dropping in from the street for a look around."

The bartender opened his mouth for an ill-natured retort, and then closed it suddenly as he recognized Wayne. He muttered something under his breath and turned away quickly.

Wayne dropped an elbow on the bar and looked the room over again. His eyes were becoming accustomed to the sting of the smoke now, and he paused in his slow survey to study the shoulders and back of the head of a man sitting alone at a table near the rear. He was thickly built and conservatively dressed, and past the lobe of his left ear Wayne could see half an inch of gray ash on the end of a cigar.

Morgan Wayne left the bar and began threading his way between the tables toward the man. He stopped beside the table and drew out a chair and sat down opposite Elliot Carson.

The ruddy-faced attorney was chewing on the butt of his Perfecto and toying with a highball glass. His lips thinned against the cigar a trifle and his eyes narrowed when he recognized Wayne. He cleared his throat and asked, "How did you get here?"

"Just walked in through the front door," said Wayne. "Where's Hendrixon?"

Carson hesitated. He took the cigar out of his mouth and frowned at it, placed it very carefully in the center of an ash tray, and lifted his glass to sip the contents. When he put it down he asked with every appearance of honest puzzlement, "What are you up to, Wayne? Where do you fit into the picture?"

"I'm wondering the same thing about you, Carson."

"But damn it, man, who are you? What are you doing here, for instance? And what gives you the idea I know where Julius is?"

"It seems a reasonable assumption," said Wayne dryly, "since you phoned him to hurry into the city to meet you. And by the way, Carson, what took you away from the Hendrixon place in such a hurry tonight that you didn't take time to apologize to a lady for not visiting her bedroom before you beat it?"

The lawyer's ruddy complexion became mottled with patches of pallor. He wet his lips and said ponderously, "I haven't the faintest idea what you are alluding to."

"Skip it," said Wayne pleasantly. "I still want to know where Hendrixon is."

Carson got out a linen handkerchief and mopped

sweat from his forehead. "I do, too. He was to have met me here half an hour ago, as you seem to have—ah—surmised. He hasn't come yet, and frankly, I'm beginning to be worried."

"Why here? And why the sudden urge to see him when you had just parted a few hours earlier?"

"Because I'm damnably worried, Wayne." Carson picked up his cigar and puffed on it vigorously. "Your talk tonight about a plot to gain control of Durtol Drugs," he went on slowly, "coupled with certain things I learned after I reached town, made an immediate conference with Julius imperative."

"Do you often arrange your business conferences here?"

"Certainly not. But I knew I'd be tied up for a time and it wasn't certain exactly when I'd be able to make it. I thought it would be more pleasant for Julius to wait for me over a drink, so I suggested we meet here."

"Now that you've got that off your chest, why not tell me the truth?"

Attorney Carson hesitated for a long time. Then he appeared to reach a decision. "Yes," he agreed firmly. "I'm going to trust you, Wayne, and take you into my confidence." He looked around furtively to see if anyone were listening, then leaned forward and asked in a low voice:

"Does the name of Hake Derr mean anything at all to you?"

Considering that Wayne had shoved a broken whisky bottle into Derr's face just a few hours previously, he remained remarkably impassive. He said, "I've heard of him."

"Very well. Are you surprised to learn that I have good reason to suspect it was he who planned Letty Hendrixon's kidnaping this afternoon?"

"Not particularly, but I'd be interested to know how you arrived at that suspicion."

"As you will recall, Inspector Hibbs is a personal

friend of mine, and he drove back to the city with me. And by the way, Wayne," the attorney went on with a frosty smile, "I don't know yet what sort of hypnosis you used on Hibbs to get his O.K. tonight, because he refused to discuss you or anything about you while we drove in together. But that isn't important. The important point is that when we reached the city the Inspector made a routine check at headquarters on my behalf and learned that two men were definitely suspected as Letty's actual kidnapers. One had been killed in some sort of fracas, it seems, and the whole affair is quite mysterious and muddled, but the important point is that both those men have been identified as hoodlums in the employ of Hake Derr."

He paused to allow Wayne to express his surprise, and seemed disappointed when the other said nothing.

"Certainly you see the importance of that—*if* your theory of a plot to gain control of Durtol is correct. You say you've heard of Derr. Perhaps you don't know he is reputed to be one of the biggest individual importers of smuggled drugs in the city. Now do you see why the Inspector's information was important?"

"It caused you to suspect Derr of the plan to take over Durtol. Sure. I've known he was back of it for weeks. But I'm convinced there's someone else behind *him*."

"Mr. Wayne, you take the words right out of my mouth." Carson was breathing heavily and he lowered his voice still more. "Perhaps you don't know that it's rumored about town that Hake Derr and the owner of this place are partners."

"I know Derr has been sleeping upstairs with Priscilla Endicott for some time," said Wayne indifferently. "What's that got to do with it?"

"A great deal, perhaps. A *very* great deal, I'm afraid. You do appear to be exceedingly well informed," Carson went on unctuously, "but there is one further item of information that I am positive you lack. As an attorney,

I ordinarily wouldn't breathe a word about a personal and delicate matter of this sort, but I feel that circumstances will not permit me to remain silent longer."

"Do you mean John Durtol's infatuation for Priscilla, which even supersedes his penchant for virgins?"

This time Carson was thoroughly taken aback. He pursed his lips worriedly and complained, "I don't know where you get all this information, Wayne. And, since you possess it, I don't understand why you haven't acted sooner. Don't you realize the implications of all this?"

Morgan Wayne shrugged his shoulders. "That John Durtol and Hake Derr got together over Priscilla's lovely body and cooked the whole thing up? Sure. That's why I'm here. Where is Priscilla, by the way?"

"I'm sure I don't know. I've never met her, you see, and wouldn't know her by sight." The lawyer looked around the crowded room restlessly. "And I do wonder what's become of Julius. It isn't like him to be late and send no message."

"What did you think to accomplish by coming here with Julius?" demanded Wayne.

"What's that? Why, I felt we should confront the woman with our suspicions. And this Derr person also, if he is present."

"He won't be," said Wayne dryly. "He kept an appointment tonight that was long overdue. I wonder if you know exactly what happened to Lois Elling tonight," he added savagely and without warning, watching Carson narrowly as he spoke.

The lawyer blinked at him and repeated the name. "Lois . . . Elling?"

"My secretary," Wayne told him softly.

"Oh, yes. I do remember now. The one who first telephoned Julius about Letty. Did something happen to her?" He spoke with disinterest, his eyes still roving about the room.

Wayne said, "She died."

"Oh. How very sad."

There were quick, light footsteps behind Wayne, then a remembered voice speaking throatily over his head to the lawyer:

"Mr. Carson! Come upstairs at once. Something dreadful has happened."

Wayne turned his head slowly and looked up into Priscilla Endicott's lovely face as the lawyer arose.

She gasped with surprise and caught her lower lip between her teeth as she recognized Wayne. For a long moment her eyes looked down into his and the color drained away from her face. Then she gained control of herself as swiftly as she had lost it, and said in a sibilant whisper:

"You, too, Morgan Wayne. John has just killed his brother-in-law in my bedroom."

Chapter Twenty

ONCE AGAIN, Morgan Wayne climbed the narrow back stairway upward to Priscilla Endicott's apartment. Once again she preceded him on the stairway, her moving loins level with his face, the woman smell of her coming back strongly into his nostrils.

But this time another man climbed the stairway directly behind Wayne, and in the bedroom above they were awaited by two other men—one of them a corpse.

The door to Priscilla's apartment stood wide open, and bright light streamed out as they reached the top. John Durtol III sat limply in a deep chair at the far end of the room in front of chartreuse draperies. He was hunched far forward with elbows resting on his knees and his face buried in both hands. An almost empty highball glass stood on the floor beside him and he didn't look up as the trio entered the room in single file.

Wayne wasted only one glance at Durtol's dejected figure and went swiftly into the bedroom past Priscilla, who stood aside and threw him a frightened and imploring glance.

Julius Hendrixon lay on his back in the middle of the bedroom floor. There was a sharp silver paper knife in his throat, and lots of blood. His eyes were open and so was his mouth.

Wayne knelt beside him and touched one finger tentatively to the outer edge of the pool of blood on the floor. It had already started to coagulate, and he estimated that the knife must have been driven into Hendrixon's throat at least ten minutes previously. He rocked back on his heels and looked searchingly about the bedroom. There was nothing out of order, nothing different from the last time he had seen it except for the dead body.

He got up and returned to the living room.

Elliot Carson was standing flat-footed in front of John, shaking his head ponderously from side to side while the younger man stared up at him with frightened eyes and insisted in a shaky voice:

"I had to do it, Elliot. It was self-defense. Priscilla will tell you. He knew his game was up, you see, and he came up here blustering and threatening both of us. He chased Priscilla into the bedroom threatening to break her neck and then mine, and I guess I went wild. Everything was red in front of me," he went on vaguely. "I remember grabbing up the paper knife from that table near the door, and that's all I do remember. You've got to believe me!" he cried out in a thin, high-pitched voice. "You've got to help me out of this, Elliot. Think of Harriet and Letty. He's dead now and he deserved to die. But they mustn't ever know the truth. You'll have to fix it, Elliot."

While he spoke, Priscilla moved quietly to Wayne's side and caught his hand in hers. She was breathing deeply and spasmodically, her gaze fastened on John's face, and squeezed Wayne's hand desperately, like a small frightened child seeking comfort from a parent.

"You see, it was Julius all the time," she broke in swiftly when John finished. "I suspected it from things Hake said, but I never was sure whether he meant Mr. Hendrixon or you, Mr. Carson. I still didn't know this afternoon when John telephoned me to say it had happened—that Letty had been kidnaped." She shuddered violently. "Think of a father doing that to his own daughter! God! If he'd known what I know about Hake Derr . . ."

"Not his own daughter," Wayne said. "Letty was actually his stepdaughter." He turned Priscilla about to face him and demanded, "Are you two saying that Julius admitted being in the plot with Derr?"

"Oh, yes." Her green eyes were wide on his. "He knew

Mr. Carson suspected when he asked to meet him here, and he got here first and came upstairs. John was with me and we were pretty sure by that time that he was the one, and he admitted it, all right. But he still wasn't giving up. He was going to kill both John and me, you see, and then go down and tell Mr. Carson that he had confronted us and John and I were in it together with Hake. And he thought Mr. Carson would help cover up for him and get him away and that maybe the police would think we had killed each other in a lovers' quarrel."

"I'm afraid I just don't understand at all," complained the attorney helplessly. "I suspected you, John, not Julius. You and this young lady together."

"That's what he was banking on, I think," said John dully.

Wayne still held Priscilla's hand tightly and his cold blue eyes probed into the bluish depths of hers, which just that afternoon had invited him to sink into them and drown deliciously. He said in a tight voice, "You've got one hell of a lot of explaining to do, Priscilla, before I'll buy any of this. How did you get into the picture in the beginning? You were Hake Derr's woman. Don't try to deny that."

"He *thought* I was his woman," she said viciously. "I let him think so. I *made* him think it." She drew in a deep breath and pulled her hand away from Wayne's. "If you knew how I loathed him—how I cringed when he touched me!"

Wayne said coldly, "Go on. And make it good."

"Damn you, Morgan Wayne," she stormed at him. "Get down off your pedestal. You're not the only person in this world who can believe in something. There are a few other human beings who hate what Hake Derr was doing as much as you do, and who have the guts to decide to do something about smashing it." For a long instant her eyes blazed challengingly into his, then she swung about and strode across the room to stand beside John's chair.

When she turned and faced Wayne again, her chin was lifted proudly and her voice was calm. "Did you ever have a sister, Morgan Wayne? One whom you raised from childhood and who looked up to you as her mother?"

Wayne said, "No," very quietly.

"I did." Her face twisted for a moment in a spasm of pain. "We lived in Detroit," she went on tonelessly. "I sang in a night club there and supported us both, until Helen was sixteen." She drew in a long breath and her hand went down to touch John Durtol's shoulder as though she drew strength from the contact.

"That was three years ago, and Helen was developing a remarkable vocal talent and I scrimped and saved to get enough money to send her here to study with a good teacher. It took just three months in New York to ruin Helen. She was weak, I suppose. Too young to go away by herself and face the temptations here. She poured out the whole hellish story to me in a long letter she wrote and mailed just before she died. It could be duplicated by thousands of other stories if people only knew the truth," she went on bitterly. "I've learned that since I've been here—since I met Hake Derr and began adding up the little things he let drop. First there were marijuana cigarettes—just for fun at a party where all the others smoked them and Helen didn't want to appear unsophisticated by refusing. Then a friend who furnished them to her for nothing when she was discouraged with her vocal progress and felt she needed a lift. Then heroin, of course, the next inevitable step. And selling herself to men for the price of the drug she had to have. But you know all of it. Helen was no different from thousands of others. Except she was *my sister*. They pulled her body out of the East River the day before her letter reached me. I came to New York with one thought in mind—to hunt down and destroy the highest man I could reach in the business of destroying girls like Helen."

Wayne nodded somberly. He said, "You moved up fast once you reached New York."

"I let nothing stop me," she agreed just as somberly. "I left every scruple behind me in Detroit. I got an engagement here with Lon Kagle's band, and in six months I was the Gingham Girl. I owned the joint and was on my way up where I could attract Hake Derr eventually. Do you want to know exactly how I managed *that*, Morgan Wayne?"

He said, "Yes."

"Ben Orcutt owned the place." She spoke without a tremor, much as though she were discussing something that did not touch her at all. "For a half interest, I traded him—myself. He was grossly fat and had a bad heart and I encouraged him to drink a great deal more than he should. So his heart suddenly stopped beating one night."

"My dear young lady!" Elliott Carson was mopping sweat from his face as he listened. "That's an unwise admission to make. Practically a confession that you planned his death."

"I suppose I did," she told him indifferently, though her eyes still held Wayne's and it was with him that she pleaded for understanding. "I tell you I was determined that nothing should stop me. When I finally landed Hake Derr, I thought he was it. That I couldn't reach any higher. Then he began hinting about the grand coup he was planning, and I waited for bigger game. And tonight he came to me," she ended evenly, nodding her head toward the bedroom. "Both he and Hake are dead now, and I hope to God the whole rotten racket will smash to earth with them. My only regret is that I didn't actually kill either one of them."

"And all this time," said Carson wonderingly, "you

and John have been working together to get proof
against Julius. Is that correct, John?"

"That's right." He nodded eagerly.

"Why didn't you tell me any of this earlier?" Wayne
demanded of Priscilla.

"I didn't dare. I still didn't know which side you were
on. Hake didn't either, you know. He really thought
you were trying to move in and take over his racket. I
wanted to trust you this afternoon." Her voice trembled
and she moved toward him, holding out her hands, a
sob creeping into her voice. "I was ready to trust you
and tell you everything, I think. If you had stayed with
me . . . when . . ." Her voice faltered and she swallowed
hard, stopping directly in front of him and reminding
him with tear-filled eyes of the moment when she had
offered herself—when he had turned away brusquely and
denied her.

Wayne put his hands on her trembling shoulders and
drew her close to him gently. Over her head, which
settled on his breast, he told Attorney Carson:

"I agree with John that this whole thing should be
hushed up. God knows, he shouldn't have to suffer for
Julius Hendrixon's death. Take him downstairs and buy
him a drink, Carson. You and he wait there for me. I'll
take care of everything here. Don't worry about publicity. I'll arrange things so the exact circumstances of
Julius' death will never be known."

He held Priscilla gently in his arms while the older
man helped the younger to his feet and out the door.
Wayne reached out to shut it behind him, then put his
fingers beneath Priscilla's chin to lift her tear-wet face
and kiss her lips gently.

Then he said, "What do I get in payment for helping
you pull it off, darling?"

Chapter Twenty-one

HER EYES were closed as he spoke. She opened them very slowly and asked in a throaty whisper, "What do you mean, Morgan?"

He released her and turned to walk across the room and sink into the chair just vacated by John Durtol III. He lit a cigarette and lifted his eyebrows mockingly. "You're one hell of an actress, Priscilla. The big money might have come a little slower on the stage, but it would have lasted longer."

She said, "I don't know what you mean."

Wayne shrugged. "Don't you think I deserve something for letting Elliot Carson go out of here believing that John killed Julius—and believing that Julius was actually the villain in the piece instead of John?"

She swayed a trifle and wet her lips. "What makes you think a crazy thing like that?"

"I know it, my sweet. You did a fast and neat job of improvising after plunging that paper knife into Julius' throat. You couldn't let Carson know the truth, of course," he went on reflectively. "He'd never have been willing to help cover up to save *you* from a charge of murder. But his own client and friend is a different matter. Do you and John have any idea of going on with your original plan after this all blows over?"

"Our—original plan?" For the first time a note of anxiety and doubt crept into Priscilla's voice.

"It was you and John all the way," Wayne told her tiredly. "It had to be, you see. Julius simply doesn't fit. We're alone here, darling. Drop your crusading pose and forget the heart-rending sob story you told us about your sister. I like you better the other way. As you were this evening. As you really are. Mercenary and tough and ready to grab the main chance when it presents itself."

"Why do you say Julius doesn't fit?" she demanded shakily. "What reason on earth have you to doubt me?"

"Because of what happened to a girl named Lois Elling. Someone had to finger her for Hake Derr. Someone who knew her name and that she was my secretary and that I had a date with her later. That has to be you, my sweet. You admitted that John telephoned you this afternoon after Lois called them about the kidnaping. None of the others could possibly have telephoned Hake Derr in time after I left their house. Carson rode in to the city with a police inspector, and he certainly didn't stop on the way to phone Derr. Julius went upstairs to his wife as soon as John left. That leaves John and you. Don't try to deny it. If you and I are going to have anything together in the future, we'll have to start out by telling the truth."

She came toward him, her face lighting and her voice tremulously exultant. "Knowing all that, you were willing to cover up for me? You'll get rid of *him* in there and never tell that lawyer the truth?"

"I don't see why Carson needs to know." Wayne smiled up at her reassuringly. "But I expect to be well repaid for that."

She stood before him breathing deeply, excitement and desire lighting flames in her eyes. "Oh, God, Morgan Wayne," she whispered. "I knew it this afternoon. Even when you walked out on me, I still knew it. But that damned woman! I was crazy with jealousy. You can't blame me for that. You were too, weren't you? You killed Hake tonight. I know you did. We're a team, sweetheart. We think alike. I want you now. I can't wait any longer." She dropped to her knees beside him, pressing herself forward with face uplifted to him.

Wayne stood up. He said, "It's a goddamned shame what the electric chair will do to that lovely body of yours, Priscilla."

For a breathless moment she shrank back on her heels away from him. Then she laughed and got slowly to her feet, deliberately ripping her gown and slip down the front and stepping out of the torn clothing.

"Don't even joke about it," she implored him. "I'm yours. Don't you see? Look at me, Morgan Wayne. Put your arms around me."

Wayne looked at her. He sighed for what might have been and turned away from her, advising flatly over his shoulder, "Better get some clothes on. I'm calling the police."

"No! You don't mean it." She was running across the room, stumbling and grabbing at him, pleading incoherently, groveling at his feet as he plodded on grimly to the telephone.

He looked down at her with his hand on the instrument, his blue eyes hooded and features strained and set. She was the most beautiful thing he had ever seen. He desired her at that moment as he had never desired another woman in his life. He said, "As God is my judge, Priscilla, I'm going to go through life hating myself for this. But I'd hate myself more every time I thought of Lois Elling if I didn't do it. You've been the direct cause of five deaths this evening," he went on harshly. "Four of them didn't matter so much, but you'll have to pay for the fifth. Hell, you may not get the chair," he went on angrily. "They may let you off with life." Again he started to lift the receiver, but Priscilla was crouched against him like an animal, sobbing wildly and attempting to climb up his legs.

"No, no," she moaned. "I can't rot away in a cell. I'd rather *die*. Do you hear me? Why should I live anyway if I can't have you? I swear before God you're the only man I ever loved. Ever wanted. You have to believe that, Morgan Wayne. That's why I told Hake to do it."

She pulled herself to her feet and stood facing him with her features contorted and swollen. "No matter

what happens to me, believe that. I don't mind dying so
much if you'll just believe me."

Wayne looked at her and said, "I do believe you." He
reached in his pocket and withdrew a short-barreled
gun, offered it to her butt forward. "There's this al-
ternative," he told her gently, "because you see, my
dear, I love you, too."

Silence was heavy in the room. She gazed down at the
offered gun, and then lifted misty eyes to his. She whispered unsteadily, "Will you kiss me once more?"

Wayne kissed her. Her lips were hot and pliable beneath his. She shuddered violently, and it was she who
drew away from him. She took the gun from his hand
without saying anything.

Wayne turned away from her and started toward the
outer door. In a frightened and choked voice behind
him, she asked, "How do you know I won't shoot you
instead?"

He continued toward the door and threw savagely
over his shoulder, "I won't have to look at myself in the
mirror tomorrow if you do."

He had his hand on the knob when a muffled ex-
plosion sounded behind him, the sound that is made
when the muzzle of a revolver is thrust inside one's mouth
before the trigger is pulled.

Wayne stood for a moment with his hand gripping
the knob so tightly that the knuckles turned white. Then
he opened the door and went out without looking back.

It would provide the police with a nice little puzzle in
deduction, he thought wearily, when they made a bal-
listics test on the bullet that had killed Priscilla and
discovered it matched the one that had killed one of
Letty's kidnapers and also the one in The Barber's head.

He didn't think it mattered that John Durtol III was
to go unsuspected of his weak part in the underworld
plot to seize the drug company. Knowing Priscilla,
Wayne was convinced she had been the driving force

behind the affair, and that John was exceedingly unlikely to deviate again.

He went steadily down the stairs and found them
seated together at a rear table with untasted drinks in
front of them. They looked up at him with strained and
expectant faces as he stopped beside the table, and Carson asked hoarsely, "Is everything all right?"

"Everything," Wayne told him flatly, "is fixed. You
two get out of here and forget everything that happened
tonight."

He swung away and strode across the now almost
empty room, past the little hat-check girl without seeing
her, and up three steps to the sidewalk and the comparatively clean night air of New York.

The doorman saw him and hurried obsequiously to
open the door of the Hudson for him, but Wayne turned
away without speaking and plodded down the sidewalk.
Let the Hudson remain standing there, he thought
wearily, to provide the police with another inexplicable
piece in the puzzle that wouldn't fit with any of the
other pieces they had.

The sidewalks of midtown New York are lonely and
deserted at four o'clock in the morning, and Morgan
Wayne was the loneliest man who walked them as he left
the Gingham Gardens behind and went blindly into the
night.

An empty taxi came cruising along the street behind
him, slowed and eased in invitingly to the curb when
the headlights picked out the lone figure on the sidewalk.

Wayne started to wave the driver on, then shrugged
and turned to open the door and get inside. It was use-
less to go on brooding over what was past. The Gingham Gardens and the Gingham Girl were behind him,
and this was tomorrow. For a month, now, he had kept
himself carefully out of sight, avoiding his former haunts
and everyone who knew him, carrying on his quixotic
one-man crusade to prevent control of a vast new source

of narcotics passing into the hands of the underworld.

For a month he had been out of touch with the world, unavailable to anyone who might have wished to contact him. It was time, now, to re-establish those severed contacts.

Though it was now past four o'clock, the Forty-One Club would still be discreetly open to welcome those habitués known personally to the owner, and Wayne felt a certain eagerness taking possession of him as he gave the address to the driver. If he were needed elsewhere, if there had been important messages for him during the past month, they would be waiting for him at 41.

After a drive of only a few blocks, the driver pulled up in the center of a dimly lighted crosstown block and looked back curiously to ask his passenger, "This the place you want, Mac?"

Morgan Wayne nodded and pushed a dollar bill over the back of the seat and got out. A short flight of wooden stairs led up from the sidewalk to double oak doors that were closed and which bore only the numerals 41. Wide windows on each side of the doors were heavily curtained and showed no light.

Wayne turned the knob and opened the unlocked door onto a small, bare vestibule lighted only with a very dim bulb in the ceiling. He closed the outer door firmly before crossing the vestibule and opening the inner door onto a large, brilliantly lighted room that had the appearance of the lounge room of a private club, furnished with comfortable leather chairs and smoking stands and with damask-covered tables ranged around three sides that would accommodate half a hundred diners.

The fourth side of the room was occupied by a long serving bar with two white-jacketed bartenders serving up drinks for the half-dozen waiters attending the wants of the special customers who had lingered convivially to this early hour.

A beaming headwaiter in immaculate white tie and

tails accosted Wayne as he entered. "Meestair Wayne. We 'ave wondered w'ere you are thees long time. Even tonight, Meestair Langdon he 'ave asked, 'Henri, 'ave you seen the Meestair Wayne thees days?' an' I 'ave tell heem—" He broke off with a slight bow as a chubby, florid-faced man in a brown, pin-striped business suit came toward them. "But 'ere ees Meestair Langdon now, to welcome you. One cognac *fine,* monsieur."

"Bring the decanter, Henri," Wayne said, and added speculatively, "Criozet Anniversaire?"

"Oui, monsieur. One decanter of Baccarat glass there ees set aside for your return." The headwaiter scurried away as the proprietor came up with a quiet smile.

"Morgan Wayne. Where've you been hiding yourself?"

Wayne shook hands with Myron Langdon and asked, "Have there been inquiries?"

"Several phone calls from Washington about two weeks ago. And Vienna has been trying for you by transatlantic telephone since midnight. You are urgently requested to call Operator Seventeen the moment you show up, though I told them I didn't have the faintest idea whether you were in New York or Calcutta."

Wayne nodded and said, "I'd better take that call in your office." He followed Langdon to the rear and through a door into a small office, where the proprietor left him alone. Wayne got long-distance and asked for Overseas operator Seventeen, gave his name, and was told rather excitedly, "Please hold on, Mr. Wayne. A call is just coming through."

Morgan Wayne held on, his face masklike, and presently, cutting through the clickings and ghostlike asides of disembodied voices, a familiar and incisive tone came clearly over the wire:

"Wayne? Are you there, Morg?"

"That you, Matt?" Wayne settled back with a grin. "I head you were top brass, but what's this Vienna deal?"

"That'll take some telling. Where the devil have you

been hiding, Morg? I got Washington on your trail two weeks ago, but no luck."

"A little thing I got tied up with," Wayne said carefully. "What's on your mind?"

"You. And the Balkans."

Wayne said, "The Balkans, Matt?"

"There's a plane waiting at La Guardia," the voice went on. "They've been standing by since midnight. I don't care what you're tied up with there . . ."

"I'm not," Wayne said curtly. "Is this official?"

"Not after you reach Budapest. From that moment, you're on your own. If there's real trouble, you're just a millionaire nitwit with a yen for adventure. And if you pull it off, you'll never be named in official citations. Can we count on you, Morg?"

"If you doubted it," said Wayne dryly, "you wouldn't be on the wire."

There was the ghost of a chuckle over the wire. "This is a woman, my boy. A woman called Z. Do you still want it?"

Wayne's features tightened. "Zelia?" he asked sharply.

"Right. That plane is waiting, Morg. I'll contact La Guardia and tell them to expect you in half an hour." There was an abrupt click and the transatlantic connection was broken.

Morgan Wayne got up slowly and went to the door. He moved across the room past the bar and shook his head firmly at Henri, who waited proudly with a decanter of Croizet Anniversaire on a tray with a large snifter of the same delicate Baccarat glass.

He said lightly, "Put it away, Henri. I'll be back before too long . . . from Budapest." He touched Henri on the shoulder and went out of 41 to hail a taxi that would take him to the airplane awaiting him at the airport.

THE END

www.ingramcontent.com/pod-product-compliance
Lightning Source LLC
Chambersburg PA
CBHW020641180626
46816CB00003B/1066